## STRANGERS IN THE NIGHT

Captain Gringo heard his tent flap open. He couldn't see who'd entered, but he assumed it was Gaston. So he was surprised when whoever it was got under the sheet with him, naked!

He took whoever she was in his arms, since he couldn't think of any better way to greet her. She snuggled closer to whisper, "I'm so frightened! What was that dreadful noise just now?"

He said, "Jaguar."

"Sir!" she suddenly exclaimed. "What on earth are you doing to my privates? Do you always rape helpless women who think they can trust you?"

"Every chance I get," he replied huskily.

"This is so humiliating and . . . uh . . . could you move a little faster, you brute?"

## Novels by
## Ramsay Thorne

## Published by
## WARNER BOOKS

# Renegade #19

# HELLFIRE
# IN
# HONDURAS

# Ramsay Thorne

WARNER BOOKS

A Warner Communications Company

WARNER BOOKS EDITION

Warner Books, Inc.,
666 Fifth Avenue,
New York, N.Y. 10103

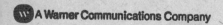 A Warner Communications Company

Printed in the United States of America

First Warner Printing: July, 1983

10  9  8  7  6  5  4  3  2  1

# Renegade #19

# HELLFIRE
# IN
# HONDURAS

Captain Gringo awakened with a start, rolled off his bunk with his pillow gun, and wound up prone, naked, armed, and dangerous in the dark before he was fully awake. He lay with his weight on his elbows, both hands gripping the double-action .38 trained on the stateroom door. His heart pounded against the hard decking as he strained with all his senses to determine what the hell he was doing down on the floor. He hadn't been dreaming. So something else must have gone bump in the night. But what?

There was a sliver of lamplight under his stateroom door. Said door had been locked from the inside before he'd turned in, but nobody seemed to be out in the companionway close enough to matter. He recalled that the companionway lamp was on the bulkhead opposite his stateroom. Feet cast shadows, and there were no shadows, so what was left?

He listened, holding his breath. Save for his own heartbeat, all he heard were the usual creakings of a rusty old tramp steamer under way. He shook his head again and muttered, "I must be getting Fugitive Fever. It's my own fault for going to bed alone and sober!"

He climbed back onto the bunk, placing the gun on the crumpled linens beside him as he groped in the dark for his shirt and a smoke. He glanced idly at the small porthole across the way, wondering what time it was. Then the penny dropped.

He muttered, "What the hell?" as he realized what had awakened him. He hadn't heard any additional bumps in the night. In fact, he had awakened because he had heard *too few*. When he'd turned in, the rusty old tub had been threatening to pop the last of the rivets holding her together as they'd wallowed south in the ground swells of the trade winds. Now they were steaming smooth as silk. Ergo, they were no longer standing out to sea. So where the hell *were* they?

Captain Gringo picked up his shirt, fished out a Havana claro and a box of wax matches, and lit up before he rose to go to the porthole. He hadn't thought to worry about that side of the tiny stateroom before, since the porthole opened out the sheer side of the hull, amidships. As he peered out, he swore softly. Harbor lights were something a guy had to swear at, this far north. He and his sidekick, Gaston, were wanted in every port north of Limón. They'd been off Honduras when he'd turned in for the night. There was no way this tub could have steamed six hundred sea miles since midnight!

The deal Gaston had made with the French purser had not included putting in this side of Costa Rica. Gaston had assured Captain Gringo that the purser of this rust bucket was an old pal from the Legion who knew the facts of life, and they'd paid the son of a bitch double the going rate.

Captain Gringo pressed his nose to the glass as he studied the ominous noose of shore lights they were steaming into. One harbor looked much like any other at night. Wherever they were, they were in trouble.

He took a deep drag on his cigar and used the glowing tip to light the oil lamp over the bunk. Then he dressed, pronto. He'd just slipped his linen jacket on over the gun he'd put back in its shoulder rig when he heard Gaston's knock.

He opened the stateroom door, and as the older, smaller soldier of fortune slipped in, Captain Gringo said, "I noticed. I thought you said we could trust these sons of bitches!"

Gaston sat down and sighed. *"Merde alors*, one would be a fool to trust his mother if she ever read all the reward posters out on the two of us. But I don't think it's that, Dick. I have enough on the rogues on the bridge of this thrice-accursed vessel to assure their joining us in durance vile. I just came from the bridge. They say the problem is salt water."

"They say *what?* We were just steaming down the *Caribbean,* you idiot!"

"Ah, you noticed that, Dick? The problem is not the salt in the sea. This species of a rusty antique has salt water in her boilers, too. Don't look at me like so. I assure you *I* didn't turn the wrong valve. I don't even know why a steam engine can't run on salt water."

Captain Gringo grimaced and said, "I do. If we're boiling brine, we're lucky to be moving at all. The damned condenser tubes must have finally rusted through. I told you when we boarded this tub in Mexico that it looked like nobody'd so much as swabbed the deck since it was launched, God knows when!"

As if to make his point, an added hush fell over the hitherto throbbing vessel. Gaston cocked an eyebrow and said, "The engines have stopped, *non?"*

"The engines have stopped, yes. We're losing headway already. But the skipper turned in soon enough to keep from going dead in the water out on the bounding main. Do you have any idea where the hell we are, by the way?"

Gaston nodded and said, *"Oui.* Puerto Cabezas."

"Jesus, Puerto Cabezas, *Nicaragua?"*

*"Sacrebleu,* don't look at me like that, Dick. I told you I didn't do it! Look at the bright side, my tall tanned youth with glowering eyes of gray. Puerto Cabezas is just south of the Nicaraguan border. A sixty-mile moonlight romp through the jungles of the adorable Mosquito Coast would see us safely across the Rio Segovia, running *très amuse* through the jungles of Honduras, *hein?"*

"For God's sake, we're wanted in Honduras, too!"

"True, but not as badly as in Nicaragua. I told you as we last left Nicaragua that they would never forgive you for sinking that gunboat so noisily, *hein?* If we can make it to Laguna Caratasca, up the Honduran coast, I used to know some rogues there who would no doubt take us in. Coastal pirates can always use extra hands who know which end of a gun the bullets come out, *non?"*

Captain Gringo moved back to the port as he asked, "How long back did you say it was when you knew these knock-around guys, Gaston?"

Gaston shrugged and said, "Ten, maybe twelve years ago. Piracy is not my usual line of work. But any old port in a storm is better than the one we seem to be in at the moment, *non?"*

Captain Gringo looked out and said, "Shit, we're dead in the water and a tug's coming out to take us in tow. That'll mean customs officials about to board. We'd better get out on deck where a guy can duck more than one way."

They stepped out into the companionway, saw nobody in sight, and moved up a ladder. Their supercargo staterooms had been booked under the midships of the three-island freighter, so when they got topside, they were in the dark by the funnel, aft of the bridge superstructure. Two lifeboats hung at either side of the funnel. So they were covered by the dark shadows aft the bridge while gaining a bird's-eye view of the dismal scene below. A couple of guys in white uniforms stood in the bow of the tug as it approached the steamer. Captain Gringo muttered, "What did I tell you? Those are customs officials, sure as hell!"

Gaston shrugged and said, *"Eh bien,* our friends in the crew are old hands at dealing with customs in strange ports. We are not in our staterooms. Our passages will hardly be engraved in stone on the ship's no-doubt-quite-in-order papers. Since we did not put in here to discharge any cargo, there is no need for anyone to make a *très fatigue* search of the whole vessel, *hein?"*

"I hope you're right. Let's talk about pirates again. Even down here, piracy seems to be a pretty obsolete industry. Didn't the British navy go boom boom a lot at some coast pirates off the Half Moon Reefs a few years ago?"

*"Oui.* I read the names of the men they hanged. None of them were anyone I ever worked with."

"I'm so happy for you. The point is that the Half Moons are just east of Laguna Caratasca, and there's been no piracy in that neighborhood since. What would these old pals of yours be doing there now—gathering Spanish moss for drinking money?"

*"Merde alors,* how should I know? I told you I haven't dropped by for supper in the last ten years. I agree they may not be there now. But do you have somewhere more important to go?"

"Let's move behind the funnel. Those shits are sure to come up on the bridge, if only to strut their stuff. We could probably take that tug over. The top of her cabin's too far to jump, but if we worked our way down to the cargo deck . . ."

Gaston waited until they were hidden in the shadow of the funnel before he sighed and said, "Behave yourself, you naughty child! I am *très* certain you could seize that poor little steam tug. I've seen you seize everything from a railroad train to a balloon since I made the mistake of escaping that firing squad with you. But leave that tug alone. There's nowhere to go in a shallow-draft vessel from here. I know this harbor. It is *très* small and *très* land-locked. Our best chance is to—"

"Hush! They're coming topside!" the tall blond American cut in, drawing his .38 with one hand as he snuffed his smoke with the other.

Gaston murmured, "Good thinking. Why should there be smoke from the vicinity of a dead funnel, *non?*"

"Will you shut up? They're on the bridge, talking to the skipper!"

Gaston drew his own pistol, silently for a change. As the two soldiers of fortune crouched in the shadows, straining their ears, they couldn't make out the words, but the conversation up ahead didn't sound excited.

A million years went by. Then they heard the familiar bustle of crewmen making ready for a tow. Captain Gringo hissed, "Cover me!" and crabbed over between the lifeboats. Nothing happened topside, so he peeked over the side, and, sure enough, the two guys in white were back aboard the tug. They were standing on the fan deck, watching with idle interest as the smaller vessel took the crippled tramp in tow. Gaston joined him, had his own peek, and said, *"Eh bien,* all is well that does not end *très fatigue.* We have been exciting ourselves over nothing, my old and nervous. They have bought our adorable skipper's story, since it is mostly true in the first place. Shall we join him and find out how long we shall have to stay here?"

Captain Gringo thought, nodded, and put his gun away. Gaston did the same before leading the way to the bridge via a hatchway opening on the deck they'd climbed to.

The skipper was not on the bridge. But Gaston knew the French watch officer as well or better. Captain Gringo listened, bemused, as the two of them spoke machine-gun French too fast for him to follow. His Spanish had gotten pretty good since he'd first jumped the U.S. border just ahead of a U.S. Army hangman. High-school French worked only when people spoke slowly. Unfortunately, he'd yet to meet a Frenchman who did.

Gaston swore in French that Captain Gringo could understand, since in their travels he called lots of people motherfuckers. Gaston turned from the watch officer and told Captain Gringo, "All is lost. For the moment they have satisfied the local authorities. But we are putting into a shipyard for extensive repairs. This offspring of an unfortunate incestuous union of halfwits tells me that the captain applied for permission to give his entire crew shore leave while this bucket of rusty bolts waits for spare parts from New Orleans."

Captain Gringo nodded soberly and said, "Right. If we stay aboard, some nosy Nicaraguan is going to wonder why. It's almost four o'clock, and the sun will be up long before we could leg it far enough to matter, even if I liked the idea of running for a hideout that might not be there anymore. We'd better hole up ashore and hope for another boat out."

Gaston grimaced and said, "Very funny. Puerto Cabezas is an out-of-the-way port of call and one could kick one of your silly *Yanqui* footballs the length of the main street."

"Okay, since you know the place so well, do you know a nice hotel with hot and cold running no-questions?"

Gaston thought, shrugged, and said, *"Oui,* but I was hoping to spend at least some of that loot from Mexico on the good things of life in Costa Rica. Bribery is *très* expensive in Nicaragua these days. The unpopular current government pays its police informers well above the usual rates."

Gaston started to move on. They were alone in a companionway by this time. Captain Gringo grabbed his arm and said, "Hold it. There's nothing in our staterooms we can't replace. We're packing our money belts and guns."

*"Oui,* but the staterooms have doors that lock. As we put in, a swarm of Nicaraguans are going to swarm aboard, *non?"*

"Exactly. Let's move down to the cargo deck. It's dark. There's bound to be a certain amount of confusion. So we slip ashore before anyone can get around to questioning us and . . ."

"But, Dick, the purser owes us. Our deal with him was passage to Limón, where neither of us are wanted by the *très fatigue* law."

"So? We're two-thirds of the way there, and we don't have to let the son of a bitch in on any future plans. You may be right about him not turning us in for the rewards aboard this tub. But make him mad, then go ashore, and what does he have to lose?"

"*Merde alors,* don't you mean what does he have to *gain? Eh bien,* I kiss my lovely Mexican gold *adieu.* But I must say, travel seems *très* expensive down here these days."

The "hotel" Gaston remembered from his last run through Puerto Cabezas wasn't exactly a hotel, or even a posada. It was a waterfront whorehouse. Captain Gringo said he should have known.

The tall American waited in the parlor downstairs while Gaston made a deal with the French Creole madam in her "office." Captain Gringo sat in a corner trying to look invisible. It wasn't easy. He had to take off his sombrero, and not another guy in the place was a gray-eyed blond with obviously Anglo-Saxon features. On the other hand, some of the working girls were blondes, thanks to peroxide, and the local males seemed more interested in dames of any color or complexion, so what the hell.

There were six or eight johns and a dozen whores lounging around among the red velvet settees, potted rubber plants, and brass cuspidors. The guys all wore the white linens of reasonably prosperous gents in these parts. The whores wore next to nothing, with lots of black lace and/or red sateen. A rinky-tink piano was playing ragtime in a corner by the small bar. Both the piano player and the barkeep were female, black, and not wearing much more than were their working sisters. A couple of the latter were giving Captain Gringo the eye as he sat there smoking a cigar and trying to look innocent. He mostly felt dumb. What in the hell was keeping Gaston? The little Frenchman had been alone with that shopworn old redhead a lot longer than it took to say yes or no.

A *muchacha* with iced-tea skin and lemonade hair came over to sit on the arm of his red velvet chair. Her face was fair, her body was fantastic. She must have been proud of it. She was wearing only black mesh stockings, and she wasn't really blond all over. She smiled down at Captain Gringo and asked, "What are we drinking, *querido?*"

He said, "If I order us gin and tonic, the barkeep won't have to put tea in your water. But all I have on me is Mexican money. Can do?"

"Is it paper or silver, *querido?*"

"Gold. My smallest change is a twenty-peso gold piece."

The whore laughed and said, "For that you can get drunk as well as laid in this place, good-looking. I am called Armida, and remember, I saw you first. Do you really need a drink to get up your courage with me? I hate to see a big spender throw his money away on club soda, but you can't drink here alone."

He said he understood the rules of the game as he fished out a coin and handed it to her. She shrugged and moved over to the bar, wiggling her bare brown rump more than she really needed to in those high heels. Captain Gringo took out his watch. Gaston had been gone nearly an hour, damn his horny hide. All but one of the guys who'd been there in the parlor when he'd first sat down had gone up to the cribs. The one guy who was still there was across the room, pretending to read a newspaper. None of the whores had joined him. He either had V.D. or, more likely, had to be the professor, or a cop. He didn't look big enough to bounce anyone. Nobody but a cop would be allowed to fall back on that bulge under his left armpit. Was there a telephone in the hall outside? Captain Gringo thought back, decided he'd have noticed if there was an easy way to call police headquarters from here, and tried to relax. If the guy was a cop, it was just as likely he'd come to see the madam for a payoff. He was probably wondering what was keeping her all this time, too.

Armida came back with two glasses filled with tepid liquid. His really had a little gin in it. The tonic water had gone flat. Ice was a semimythical, exotic substance in a tropic dive like this. They had one of those new electric ceiling fans, moving sluggishly above. It was still too hot even to think about sex, even if he'd been in the habit of paying for it. But Armida leaned to brush a nipple against his ear as she husked, "Now that we have our drinks, what say we go upstairs, eh?"

He said, "Not just yet. I'm waiting for someone. I don't suppose there was any change, huh?"

"Why do you want change, big spender? I told you you'd paid for me as well as the drinks."

He was too polite to point out that she couldn't be worth half that much, and, what the hell, he'd stolen the gold pesos. The guy across the way was staring over the top of his paper, eyes opaque. He wasn't looking at them in particular, but he didn't seem to be missing much. Captain Gringo slid his free hand around the Mestiza's naked waist to satisfy the stranger's curiosity as he told her, again, "I have to stay here until my *compañero* finishes with your madam, *querida.*"

She chuckled and said, "They've been alone in there long enough to do it all three ways, twice. They must be old friends. Madam Fifi seldom entertains customers herself. You say you *hombres* just came down from Mexico?"

He hadn't, but the coin he'd given her had. He said, "I won some pesos playing cards the other night. My amigo and me are from Costa Rica."

The whore laughed and said, "No, you're not. If you are not a gringo, I am the Queen of England. But I understand. We get lots of your sort here. Is it not fortunate that Costa Rica is one of the few countries that has no extradition treaty with Tío Sam?"

He felt her up, absently, as he smiled sheepishly and said, "I heard you people here were understanding, Armida. As long as we're on the subject, who's that *hombre* over there behind the newspaper, a cop?"

She shook her bleached head slightly and said, "Not a cop. Don't ask any more about him. He won't ask about you. Rules of the house."

"I like your rules, Armida."

"You seem to like my ass, too. I told you it was yours for the taking, but for God's sake let's do it upstairs. Madam allows no shocking behavior down here in the parlor, and you have a shocking finger against my asshole. Are you trying to warm me up for Greek loving? *Bueno*, I am game, unless you are as big all over. Shoulders like yours can worry a girl!"

He doubted she'd be worried by a well-hung stallion. But he raised his hand to the small of her back, anyway. He knew she was trying to get him hot. The hell of it was, he was. He'd thought when he parted company with that big dumb Yankee gal in Nuevo Santiago that he wouldn't want to see another snatch for at least a month. But the long slow sea voyage had done wonders for his health, and it was hard to remember his own rules while running his hands over well-stacked naked female flesh.

He'd paid for it in his time. Any man over twenty-one who hadn't tried at least one whore was probably a prude. But he'd never really enjoyed a whore, unless she put out for free. Gaston accused him of having a *très fatigue romantique* nature. Gaston was probably right. But it sure felt dumb to bounce up and down on a dame who was doubtless thinking about something else, once you'd paid her.

He fumbled a sip from his glass with the cigar held awkwardly in the same hand, since the other was busy. Armida took the cigar, puffed it sensually, and said, "You are going to burn your eyebrows. Would you like to see me smoke this with my pussy?"

"Not hardly; it's an expensive cigar. I thought you said you weren't supposed to do anything shocking down here."

"Silly, I meant upstairs. Listen, if you let me have all the change from these drinks, I am yours all day. *La siesta* will be starting soon, and most of our customers are required to go home and reassure their wives during *la siesta*. I can smoke with my rectum, too. I have fantastic control of my love muscles."

His own love muscles were getting out of control indeed, even though he knew he was supposed to feel disgusted by this little waterfront bawd. What the hell, she was younger than he, so how many more times than he could she have changed partners, right? She apparently liked him, and it wasn't as if he'd paid her, exactly. He knew he'd never get his change back without wrecking the joint, whether he took her brown ass in trade or not.

Then Gaston came into the parlor, looking tired but rather pleased with himself. The little Frenchman moved his head to signal a move to the bar. Captain Gringo told Armida he'd see her around the campus and got up to join Gaston. Armida was too smart to follow.

As the two soldiers of fortune bellied up to the bar together, Captain Gringo muttered, "It's about time. How many times did you come in that old pig?"

Gaston chuckled and replied, "Now, Dick, is that any way to talk about our landlady? We are, as you say, all set. Aside from being happy to see an old friend, Fifi is a member of the Conservative party."

Captain Gringo started to ask a dumb question. Then he remembered that the so-called Nicaraguan Liberal party had won the last revolution. The names meant nothing. The Liberals were a bunch of totalitarian militarists, and the so-called Conservatives were another, who weren't related to them closely enough to get on the public payroll. The little people on both sides had been screwed, so why they fought for either eluded Captain Gringo, but it wasn't his country so it wasn't his problem.

Gaston said, "I hope you didn't pay for that drink. Now that Fifi and I have resumed our, ah, companionship, everything is on the house. We have a couple of cribs upstairs. Sanitary facilities should be amusing, since we share the bathroom down the hall with *les* girls. Fifi says she will send food up to us privately. I don't think we should spend too much time down here among the customers, *hein?*"

"When you're right you're right, Gaston. But are you saying you didn't have to give the madam anything?"

*"Merde alors,* I gave her my all, and had to eat her, too! She did accept a hundred pesos, graciously, but had I not made her come, to her considerable surprise and delight . . ."

"Never mind your sex life. I can see you're fixed up, and I'm more worried about getting back to our base in Costa Rica. What did she say about a ship out of here?"

*"Merde alors,* what could she say? As you see, Fifi sells booze and broads, not steamship tickets. This is a whorehouse, not a travel agency."

"I noticed that. Look, Gaston, not even your dicking is going to keep us here indefinitely, and you were right about it being a small dull town, outside. Let's say we have, oh, seventy-two hours before Madam Fifi has her fill of you. Then what?"

Gaston shrugged and answered, "I can usually keep most women satisfied a month before they start nagging me about not having a steady job and telling me I am only using them. That is why they call it the honeymoon."

The tall American sighed and said, "I think I must have dated their kid sisters. But whores have even shorter attention spans, Gaston. There's no way we can stay here more than a day or so."

The black barkeep slid down to them. Gaston ordered two more gin and tonics and said it was on the house. The black girl said Madam Fifi hadn't said anything about that to her. As Gaston swore and put a coin on the bar, Captain Gringo said, "See what I mean? You'd better put on your cape of invisibility and start scouting up at least a southbound fishing boat."

Gaston sipped his drink, grimaced at all the water in it, and replied, *"Eh bien,* I learned in my youth never to trust a place that waters drinks. I'll go out after *la siesta.* Even us small gray cats draw a certain amount of attention when the streets are deserted. Let us take a bottle along with these glasses as we climb the stairs, *hein?* Fifi said she might be joining me for a siesta, and a man my age needs to keep up his strength."

Captain Gringo asked the black girl for a bottle of gin. When she slid it across the mahogany, he said, "Take it out of the change you forgot to give me before."

She frowned and asked, "Aren't you paying Armida?"

"For what? She's talking to another john now, and that was a twenty-peso gold piece I gave you, doll!"

He turned away with the bottle and Gaston before she could bitch about it. As they left, Armida shot Captain Gringo a hurt look from where she sat in another man's lap, bare-assed.

They went upstairs. Gaston started counting off the numbers as they passed the close-set doors on either side. He nodded and said, *"Eh bien,* here we are. This one's mine. Yours is next door, Dick."

"Don't we get keys?"

"In a whorehouse? Surely you jest. Hopefully there are barrel bolts inside. Fifi says these cribs are not currently in use, so, hopefully, we don't have to worry about the linen."

A door down the hall opened and a tipsy fat man came out, buttoning his pants. By unspoken agreement the two soldiers of fortune made themselves scarce by ducking into their respective cribs.

Captain Gringo found his small, paneled with white-enameled pine, and already crowded as he stood in the narrow space by the bed, which took up most of the room. There was a narrow jalousied window. He opened the slats to see a blank stucco wall staring him in the face across a narrow alley. He didn't think he could get out through such a narrow slot in any case. He left the slats open to have some light on the subject.

He closed the door. It had once had an inside bolt, but someone had kicked the door in at one time. The brass hardware had never been replaced, and he saw nothing he could prop against the door.

Save for the brass bedstead, the only furniture was an end table improvised from a packing crate. There were hooks on the walls and an Edison bulb hanging from the ceiling on a threadbare wire. Since it was still early, it wasn't important whether the light worked. The idea of spending a whole night here, dark or otherwise, was too grim to contemplate. So he didn't.

He took off his hat and jacket and hung them up. It didn't help much. Even with the jalousies open it was hot and stuffy. He pulled down the bed covers. The linen looked clean. He took off his gun rig and slid his hardware under the pillow. Then he sat down on the bed, wondering what the hell he was going to do for the rest of the day.

His smoke was about gone. He snuffed out the claro in a tin tray on the end table and didn't light another. He sipped one of the two glasses he'd brought from the bar. Where the hell was the bottle? Oh, yeah, Gaston had taken it on the way up. Gaston was like that. But once the streets were safe again, nobody could beat Gaston at moving around unobserved. Gaston didn't sneak. He was too old a hand at invisibility to pussy-foot. Gaston took advantage of the fact that nobody seemed to notice a small middle-aged guy unless he made sudden moves. The little Frenchman's Spanish was letter perfect and he could pass for a native in most Latin ports.

If there was a southbound vessel with an understanding purser in Puerto Cabezas, Gaston would find it. If there wasn't . . . then what? That run for the old pirate base in Honduras sounded lousy. Running in any other direction sounded worse. The last time they'd been here in Nicaragua they'd been fighting for the side that lost. The winning side had an awesome reward posted on the two of them, dead or otherwise, and Gaston's old playmate, Madam Fifi, would sell you her *own* ass, for small change!

He took off his shirt and hung it up. It felt so good that he took off his boots and pants as well. It was still too hot, but the starched linen felt cooler on his naked flesh as he reclined on the bed, draining the first glass and picking up the other.

The door opened and Armida came in. She must have noticed what a hot day it was getting to be, too. She'd even peeled off her mesh stockings. So they were both naked as jays when she sat down on the bed and calmly took his shaft in hand.

It was limp, of course. Captain Gringo had more delicate feelings. He grimaced and said, "That was quick, even for a pro."

She said, "Don't be vulgar. Poor Pablo never goes upstairs with any of us. He just comes to drink and listen to dirty talk before going home to his *mujer* with renewed inspiration."

Captain Gringo was feeling inspired now, too. For, despite a certain distaste for his surroundings and present company, he hadn't been getting any lately, and her strange skilled fingers on his dawning erection sure felt better than his own could have.

Nonetheless, he said, "Hold it, Armida. Before we get into a dreadful misunderstanding, it's only fair to warn you there's no more gold on its way out of my pocket."

She held it indeed as she frowned down at him and asked, "Don't you think I'm worth it?"

"You would be if I made a habit of paying. I don't mind being overcharged for booze, even when my sidekick winds up with it. But let go of my friend there while we establish some new ground rules. You see, Gaston and I are guests of Madam Fifi, not johns, and . . ."

Armida half-rose, cocked a long shapely leg over him to plant one heel on the mattress, with the other on the floor, and lowered her slit to sit herself on his raging erection, saying, "I know all about that. Madam said I was to make you comfortable and . . . Oh, *yes!* That does feel most comfortable, no?"

He hissed in pleasure, too, as she gripped hard with her internal muscles. It was obvious she'd told the truth when she'd said she could smoke a cigar with her educated pussy.

Armida moved up and down slowly with her love muscles rippling faster. She gripped him so tightly it would have chafed them both if she'd been drier inside. He was too polite to ask if her lubrication was friendship or mineral oil. It sure felt like the real thing. She leaned forward to place her palms on his heaving chest for balance. Then she started moving her pelvis astoundingly as he grinned up at her, admiring the view. Her nipples were turgid and her breasts bobbed in rhythm with her rippling lower torso muscles as she moved in a way that an Arabian belly dancer would have envied. She was literally sucking him off with her body, and he was tempted to roll her over and finish right.

But he knew she'd expect to be kissed if he got on top, and a guy had to draw the line somewhere. A whore showing off was the best there was, but he wasn't sure he wanted to kiss those painted lips without assurances she'd gargled with disinfectant since the last customer!

She moaned. "Oh, I can't believe it! I'm going to *come!* You'll ruin me for the day, you naughty thing!"

He didn't see why he should believe that. But as she fell weakly down against him, her nipples teasing his chest as her spasming love box went on milking his tool, he closed his eyes and ejaculated in her, hard.

Armida giggled and said, "I felt that. I just came, too. There's no sense going downstairs now. A working girl needs an objective attitude, and you have me hot as a blushing bride.

It's almost siesta time anyway. Would you like to spend the whole siesta in me, *querido?*"

He answered by thrusting his still-erect shaft deeper. She laughed and said, "I can't do it again on top. As a matter of fact, I need a drink before I do it again at all. Did you not say something about a bottle?"

As she sat up, arching her back to raise her arms and smooth her hair, he said, "I bought the bottle. Gaston grabbed it. All I have is what's left in that one glass."

She leaned forward, his shaft still in her, and her left breast kissed his lips as she stretched an arm to get the glass from the end table. She sat up again, took a sip, and asked him if he wanted to kill it.

He said, "Can't, in this position. Let me sit up."

Armida got off with an audible wet pop and rolled to a seated position by him as Captain Gringo sat up, took the glass, and started to drink from it. Then he sighed, smiled fondly at the treacherous blond bitch, and cold-cocked her with a left cross to the jaw.

Armida's head flew back and bounced off the pine paneling above the bed before she sprawled unconscious across it, hips on the edge of the mattress and long shapely legs spread invitingly. Captain Gringo wiped himself dry with a corner of the sheet, got to his feet, and put on his shirt and gun rig as he stared down at her pink slit wistfully and muttered, "Hell, it was just getting hot, too!"

He didn't have time to take her up on her unconscious offer. Having armed himself, he sat down again and hauled on his pants and cordovan mosquito boots. He'd just stood up to stomp his boots firmly in place when the door opened. He whipped out his .38, saw that it was Gaston, fully dressed, and said, "Don't ever do that without knocking. I was just coming for you."

Gaston smiled thinly down at the unconscious whore and said, "I see you came for *her*, too. *Eh bien*, I'm glad you smelled the chloral hydrate in time."

"So am I. She must have had the knockout pill in her hair. They gave her a dose for a whole bottle, so dropping it in half a glass of gin and tonic was a little much. It would have killed me if I'd been dumb enough to drink it!"

*"Oui,* but look at it this way, the reward says dead or alive. Madam Fifi certainly disappointed me, Dick. I am mortified to have gotten you into this."

"Let's worry about getting *out* of it. Obviously the cops are waiting for *la siesta* and an empty cathouse before they move in. That gives us, let's say, five minutes in case my watch is slow. What's the story on old Fifi?"

"The same as yours. Great minds run in the same channels, *non?* It was harder to smell her sleeping potion in a whole bottle of gin, but when one has been rolled as many times as I, one's nose develops skills the mundane john may not have. Of course I knocked her out before I left her bound and gagged next door. We'd better do the same to this one before we leave, *non?"*

Captain Gringo didn't answer as Gaston picked up the end of the sheet Armida wasn't on and proceeded to tear it into strips. The tall American was more interested in the window. He twisted his shoulders sideways and, just, managed to lean his upper body out to study the narrow slot between the buildings. By reaching out one hand, he could brace himself against the rough stucco across the alley, or air shaft, or whatever the hell it was. He decided it was just a gap left over when they'd built the joint. The ground below was covered with weeds and broken glass.

Toward the front of the whorehouse, a whitewashed wooden wall had been erected to keep drunks from coming in there to piss. Back the other way, the slot ended in the wall of an ell built out to take full advantage of the space. There was no window facing him from either direction, Allah be praised.

He ducked back inside. Gaston had tied Armida's wrists above her head to the head rails of the brass bedstead. Her eyes were open, but she couldn't say much with that linen gag in her mouth. But she was moving pretty good as Gaston lay atop her with his pants down, tearing off a piece.

Captain Gringo laughed incredulously and asked, "What the fuck are you doing? You sure have a grotesque sense of timing, Gaston."

"I'll be with you in a moment, M'sieur. I had to knock Fifi out in the middle of a blow job and I can't run fast with an erection."

He went on raping the whore, if rape was the right term, as he added, conversationally, "What is the story outside? Ah, it's very nice in *here,* and . . . *Voilà!* I am satisfied, for the moment."

"Pull your goddamn pants up and get over here. There's no way I'd ever be able to draw while oozing through this skinny window. So you'd better go first and cover me."

"*Eh bien,* but what about these two ladies we must bid *adieu* so posthaste? The *très fatigue* police will ask them which way we went, and if we leave them in condition to talk . . ."

"Let 'em. Anyone can see there's only one way out. By the time anyone opens either discreetly closed door, we'll be a mile or more into the jungle. Come on, Gaston, move it!"

Gaston did. Since he was much smaller, he had no trouble sliding out the window and dropping to the weeds below from the second-story window.

As Gaston covered the wooden fence with his own revolver, Captain Gringo followed, grimacing as he scraped himself through the narrow space and cursing as he landed harder than a man his weight was supposed to.

But the two-story drop hadn't sprained anything important, and, as he picked himself up, Gaston said, "*Eh bien.* Over the fence and into the woods, to *grandmère's* house we go?"

"Don't be silly. Didn't you just hear me tell that whore that that was the plan?"

"*Oui,* I assumed it was what you wanted her to tell the police. But I am missing something here, Dick. As anyone can see, over that fence is the only way out of this narrow slot, *non?*"

Captain Gringo said, "No," and braced his back against one stucco wall as he raised a boot heel to brace against the opposite wall. As he started levering himself skyward, Gaston grinned and said, "Ah, the old roof trick. Mundane, but usually effective, when the flicks expect to find you somewhere else!"

Gaston wedged his own lighter body the same way, and, while his legs had less leverage, he had less to lift, so it tended to even out. A few minutes later the two soldiers of fortune had shimmied themselves to rooftop level. Captain Gringo beat Gaston to the whorehouse roof and reached down to haul his comrade up beside him. As they crouched atop the flat roof, Gaston pointed with his chin and said, *"Merde alors,* we could have done it the easy way! There's a triple-titted trap door over there by the chimney pots!"

"Yeah. We can't stay here. The laziest cops usually pop open a door at the top of a stairway. Let's see, now. It's an easy jump across to the building we were just kicking the shit out of. But it's got a tile roof. Too noisy. Follow me."

Gaston did, as the tall American crawled the other way, keeping his ass down. The flat roof of Madam Fifi's had a low stucco parapet, so nobody could see them from street level, but there were higher buildings in the neighborhood, and though very few people took their siesta on a rooftop under a blazing tropic sun, why take chances?

They made it to the opposite side. Captain Gringo eased his head up for a look over the parapet and said, "That's better. Next building has a flat gravel roof, too."

They rolled over the parapet. Gaston said, *"Eh bien,* if we lay low, here . . ."

"We bake like tortillas on the hearth till some wise-ass cop sticks his head over the edge. Keep *crawling,* damm it!"

They did, crossing three roofs before they came to a six- or eight-foot gap before the next building on the block. Captain Gringo said, "This must be the place. No cop's about to jump across that gap without a hell of a good reason, and the girls should tell 'em we said something about a jungle."

Gaston peered over the edge and muttered, "No Frenchman in his right mind is going to try it either! That's a three-story drop, Dick!"

"I'll go first and catch you. No running jump. People wonder about the pitty pat of tiny feet on their bedroom ceiling. Try to land on that brick parapet over there instead of the roof itself."

Gaston was still bitching when Captain Gringo stood up, mounted the parapet, and bent his knees for a standing broad jump that had to be right the first time.

He made it, just, and teetered for a frightening moment on the rim across the way before he managed to recover his balance and step down softly to safer footing. He cursed the heat, and that whore, as he recovered his relative calm. For he'd jumped that far, easier, in his West Point days.

He turned and motioned to Gaston. The little Frenchman couldn't bitch out loud, for a change, so he made the sign of the cross and tried. He almost made it. His toes hit the stucco just below the top of the parapet, and he would have dropped down the slot had Captain Gringo not caught a wildly flailing arm and hauled him safely atop the roof. Gaston muttered, "I must be getting old. At the rate you are going, I doubt I'll get much older. Have I ever told you that you are a maniac, my overactive child?"

"Many, many times. It must be the company I keep. Okay, I think that takes care of strolling cops. The next problem is finding some shade. It's damn near high noon and we're about fourteen degrees north of the equator."

"True, it would be *très* droll to suffer heat stroke instead of police bullets. But where do you suggest we go from here? As you see, we are near the end of the block. *La siesta* has started by now, and people are most surprised to see one on the streets during *la siesta,* even when they know your face."

"Good thinking. There's a shack of some kind over on the next roof. We'd better get on the far side in case some cop doesn't buy the tale we planted and decides to have a look around up here."

They moved quietly toward what seemed to be an improvised wooden hut someone had built on the flat roof of the last building on the block. As they approached, Captain Gringo muttered, "Swing left. There's a trap door to the right."

It was well that they did so. The two soldiers of fortune had just flattened out against the far side of the ramshackle structure when they heard the creak of hinges. They looked silently at each other and drew their guns in unspoken agreement. A muffled female voice called out, "Tico, why are you going up there at this hour? You will fry your brains, my son!"

A too-close-for-comfort youthful voice replied, "I have to water my pigeons, mamacita!"

"*Ay que muchacho*, leave those stupid birds alone and come down here this instant! Even pigeons know better than to go out in the hot sun at this time of day!"

"*Sí, sí, un momento*, mamacita. I just have to make sure they have water."

The two soldiers of fortune strained their ears as, on the far side of the thin wooden wall, they heard the softer sounds of baby talk and gurgling water. The woman below called out again, adding a threat to send papacito up with a switch. Tico, if that was his name, slammed the pigeon-loft door and they heard his footsteps running for the trap door. Then it slammed and they could breathe again.

Captain Gringo grinned and said, "You were looking for some shade?"

"*Oui*, but in a pigeon loft?"

"Why not? I'm sure there's room. That kid won't come back until at least three, right?"

He led the way around the side not exposed to the street and quietly opened the door. The white pigeons all around tried to bark like dogs, but all they could manage were soft, albeit angry, coos as the two of them got inside and shut the door again. The interior of the pigeon loft was about as comfortable as a Turkish bath perfumed with bird shit, but at least they were out of the sun now.

Here and there sunlight lanced through cracks in the rough planking, so they could see well enough. Gaston picked up the water olla the kid had left and helped himself to a long swig before he said, "God bless that child," and handed it to Captain Gringo.

The tall American said, "Yeah, I was already thirsty when I smelled the chloral hydrate in my glass. Don't light that smoke, you idiot!"

"Why not? I assure you I have no intention of setting one of these birds on fire."

"No, but if you stink this stuffy loft up with cigar smoke, young Tico's sure going to wonder when his pets started smoking." He took a healthy swig of tepid water, put the olla back on its shelf, and added, "We'd better leave here about two-thirty. That kid's eager about his hobby and might jump the gun on the official end of *la siesta* at three."

Gaston hunkered down with his back braced against a post and said, "That sounds sensible. But we still have a bit of a problem, Dick. In your enthusiasm, you let that whore hear you say we were running into the jungle. Ergo, the annoying people who run this distressing country will be covering all the trails out of Puerto Cabezas long before two-thirty, *non?*"

"Yeah, I never liked that idea of running off to be a pirate, anyway. I outgrew ideas like that even before Tom Sawyer did."

"I've heard of that new novel, though I have not read it. I agree a romp through the jungle would not be wise right now. You just pointed out that we can't stay here, even if one enjoyed the company of dirty birds. So where do you suggest we go, Dick?"

"Beats me. You're the guy who knows this town, Gaston."

*"Merde alors,* I told you it was small enough to kick a football across! Fifi was the only old friend I knew here, and, as you just saw, she seems to have forgotten her old friends. What if we went back to the ship? We left them in a hopefully friendly mood, and the purser still owes us."

Captain Gringo shook his head and said, "No way. Assuming the purser's an honest crook, old Fifi wasn't, so they know we're in town. The only way we could have gotten here was aboard that crippled steamer. For God's sake, do I have to draw diagrams on the blackboard for you?"

*"Mais non,* the picture emerges from the mists with distressing clarity. *Eh bien,* we can't go back to Fifi's. We can't go back to the ship. If we run for the trees, we are certain to fall into an ambush. Traveling with you is *très fatigue,* Dick. We seem to be, how you say, up *le* creek *sans* any paddle!"

"Look at the bright side. We're still *alive.* The waterfront should be crowded this evening, and nobody can see my hair if I keep this sombrero down tight. The cops will have chased our shadows through the jungle a lot by then. Hopefully, they'll give us credit for being slicker jungle runners than them and shouldn't expect to see us in town tonight."

"I give that fifty-fifty. But so what? We can mingle with the crowd until the streets are once more deserted for the night. But we don't dare try another hotel accommodation. The country's hovering on the brink of revolution, and with less than a dozen posadas to check out . . ."

"We tried a no-questions joint and it didn't turn out so hot," Captain Gringo cut in, adding, "If we can't get out by land, it'll have to be by sea."

Gaston grimaced and said, "I already considered that. There are no other steamers in port at the moment. I told you it was an out-of-the-way port of call."

"You did. I noticed a mess of fishing boats in the harbor as we came in last night, too. The two of us ought to be able to man a fishing ketch, and they can't all be guarded after dark."

Gaston shook his head in disgust and muttered, half to himself, "I really could have saved myself a *très fatigue* old age if I'd just let them shoot me that time we met in Mexico. Since I have been running through life with you, I have hardly had a good night's sleep."

"What can I tell you? You said you wanted to be a pirate when you grew up."

"*Merde alors*, grabbing a fishing ketch goes beyond mere piracy into an exercise in futility, Dick! Where in the devil do you propose we sail in our beautiful pea-green boat? We're a good three hundred miles or more from Limón, and even if the open sea doesn't kill us, even Costa Rica frowns on sailing in aboard a stolen vessel, *non?*"

Captain Gringo shrugged and said, "Jesus, what a worry wart. We haven't even stolen the boat yet and he's bitching about explaining it in Limón. Can't you see we'll probably be shipwrecked long before we get there, pal?"

They left the rooftops at two-thirty, skulked in an alley for an even less interesting time, and then went to three-o'clock Mass at a nearby church Gaston remembered. Neither of them had suddenly gotten religion. Gaston pointed out that most Nicaraguan priests belonged to the Conservative party that was currently out of power.

The reward posters out on Captain Gringo had him down as a Protestant, which might have been true, back in the days when he'd thought someone might be running this mad universe. Gaston had been born a nominal Catholic, but who looked for knock-around guys in church when the cantinas were starting to open up again for the evening?

They took a back pew, put a gold coin in the collection plate when it was passed, and nobody saw fit to bother them after Mass was over and everyone but a few old women in shawls filed out.

It was cool, quiet, and they had plenty of time to plan their next moves as they waited for the sun to go down. But when it seemed safe to leave, they still hadn't come up with anything better than Captain Gringo's plan to swipe a fishing boat, and Gaston said he was already getting sea sick.

When they left the old church the shadows were long and lavender under a flamingo sky. It was hard to make out features in the never-never light of the gloaming, and, as they'd foreseen, the streets were crowding up as the locals made ready for the nightly paseo.

The young and single of Puerto Cabezas were out for adventure in the cool of the evening. The older poor married slobs could at least watch and get drunk. Having dozed the hot afternoon away, nobody would be turning in this side of midnight unless they got lucky with a lady who had her own room. So they couldn't grab a boat until things settled down, and, despite the tricky light, there were limits to how well a tall blond Anglo-Saxon could blend into a crowd of darker, mostly shorter natives.

Captain Gringo knew he'd get in trouble if they hung around the main plaza during the paseo. With the women strolling the plaza one way, the men strolling the other, and one and all giving everyone a good looking-over as they passed, someone was sure to notice and, worse yet, comment on a tall gringo stranger in their tiny town.

Gaston knew a couple of cantinas along the waterfront. Gaston apparently had never passed a waterfront cantina south of the Tropic of Cancer without checking it out. Captain Gringo got in trouble in bars a lot, too. He asked if the Frenchman knew a quieter, darker place to hang out awhile.

Gaston lit a smoke as he keel hauled Puerto Cabezas through his memory. Then he nodded and said, "I have just the place. We can get something to eat there, too!"

That reminded Captain Gringo that he hadn't eaten all day. He said, "I'm game for anything that doesn't hurt. How far is this restaurant of yours?"

"Ah, it's not exactly a restaurant and it's hardly mine, Dick. There's a *très* expensive posada near the docks, catering mostly to foolishly rich foreigners. They serve a buffet in the deliciously dark lobby, as I recall. I can park you there while scouting up some transportation, *non?*"

Captain Gringo frowned and said, "I asked about a discreet place, not a tourist hotel, for God's sake!"

*"Eh bien*, I heard you. As I said, it's too expensive to attract the locals, or even crewmen from that steamer we just left. The beauty of my plan is that nobody is supposed to use the buffet lounge unless they are guests of the posada. Wait, I know what you are thinking. Of course one must register if one checks into the overpriced establishment. On the other hand, there is a side entrance nobody can see from the desk. How do you like it so far?"

Captain Gringo thought as he lit his own claro. Then he nodded and said, "Right, I used to do that in fancy New York hotels when I was a cadet at the Point. If you act like a guest in the lobby, everyone assumes you've checked in. Better yet, since your name's not on the register, the cops who drop by from time to time to check on mysterious new big spenders in town don't case the joint downstairs. It's easier to just leaf through the register at said desk. You say they have food on tap?"

*"Oui.* Free. The drinks in the lounge are outrageously overpriced, but nobody cares how many hors d'oeuvres one helps oneself to from the buffet, if one is not an obvious pig about it. Come, it's down this way, as I recall."

Gaston led the way toward the waterfront as Captain Gringo

got his bearings. A shot tower in the distance told him they were at the far end of town from the shipyards to which the crippled steamer had been towed. That wasn't saying much in a port this size, but hopefully the crewmen who knew their faces would find booze and broads closer to their ship.

The posada was a big rambling pile of wedding cake Spanish baroque, taking up most of a whole block. Gaston steered them into an alley well clear of the main entrance down the walk, saying, "The side door I told you about opens into this adorable dark cul-de-sac. Regard the lights ahead."

Captain Gringo did. But he was more interested in what stood parked between them and the lamp-lit windows of the lounge beyond. A big black Stanley Steamer sulked quietly on its red rubber tires, staring at them owlishly with its unlit brass headlights. As they eased between the mysterious horseless carriage and the plaster wall, he noticed that the pilot light was purring like a big cat under the long hood. He said, "Jesus, what a funny place to see a Stanley Steamer. It's parked there with a full head of steam, too."

Gaston said, "Forget it. You drive like a maniac; besides, there is no open road from this species of fishing village to anywhere at all important."

"I wasn't thinking about stealing it. I was just wondering what the hell it's doing here. Horseless carriages in a half-horse town don't make sense. A Stanley costs a bundle, too."

"*Eh bien*, perhaps there is a rich eccentric staying here. I told you they charged outrageous prices. Let us *eat*, for God's sake!"

Nobody commented when the two soldiers of fortune came in the side door and strode boldly to the bar at one end of the dimly lit lounge. The white-jacketed black barkeep served them gin and tonic, with ice, yet, and asked politely if they wanted the tabs put on their guest bills. Gaston said, calmly, that they'd better keep their room service and bar tabs separate.

When the barkeep saw the twenty-peso gold piece on the mahogany, he seemed satisfied that they weren't a couple of bums in off the street. They left him a nice tip from the change and eased over to a couple of chairs under a potted palm to give everyone a chance to get used to them being there. It wasn't easy. A long buffet table ran along the nearby wall, and the smell of all that grub was pure torture to a pair of half-starved castaways.

By tacit agreement, Gaston cased the lounge one way and Captain Gringo the other as they sat there sipping like a couple of bored rich tourists. It was just as well the light was so murky. Their planter's sombreros were acceptable headgear in these parts, but their linen suits were a mite grimy after crawling and sweating a lot that afternoon.

There were only a few other guests in the lounge. Nobody looked like anyone they had to worry about. A tall, skinny old guy with a horsey laugh was trying to pick up a dame he should have been ashamed to be seen in public with. She looked like a sparrow dressed up to become a schoolmarm. Captain Gringo doubted that the old gent was going to get anywhere with her, but neither seemed at all interested in him and Gaston, so he wished them well. Gaston cased a fat man reading a book with one hand as he drank himself to death with the other. Gaston murmured, *"Eh bien.* You stay here. I shall get us some goodies from the buffet."

He handed his glass to Captain Gringo, got up as if he'd just noticed the food, and wandered over to investigate. He kept his back to the bar as he piled two plates full of hors d'oeuvres and brought them back to base camp under the potted palm. As he handed one to Captain Gringo, the big Yank laughed and said, "I thought we weren't supposed to be piggy. There's enough here to feed an army!"

"The fewer trips the better, *non?* Besides, like most hors d'oeuvres, it's mostly air."

The assortment of pastry and cold cuts tasted good, though, and in no time they'd both cleaned their plates. Gaston suggested second helpings. Captain Gringo shook his head and said, "Wait awhile. It's too damned empty in here. That barkeep has nothing to keep him busy. What time does the action start around here?"

Gaston shrugged and said, "I am not sure it ever does. Any guest looking for a pickup would do better over at the paseo. That idiot trying to make time with the traveling spinster is obviously new to the tropics."

Captain Gringo consulted his watch and said, "It should be dark enough outside to case the waterfront now."

Gaston said, "You stay right where you are, you conspicuous moose. Since you won't let me eat seriously here, I may as well wend my weary way along the quay to see if there's a boat that is neither under guard nor in immediate danger of sinking at its moorings. I take it we desire a ketch rig, *non?*"

"Yeah, a sloop's too slow and a schooner rig's too much for us to man. If you can find one with auxiliary power I'll kiss you."

*"Merde alors,* if I can find a *fishing* boat with an *engine,* I can walk on water! Try to stay out of trouble until I get back, *hein?"*

After Gaston left, the lounge seemed even more boring. Captain Gringo nursed his drink as long as he could without being obvious. Then he bought another and, as long as he was on his feet, helped himself to another plate of grub. But after a guy drinks, eats, and smokes for a couple of hours, potted palms get mighty uninteresting to look at, and that silly laugh from the idiot down at the far end was beginning to affect him like fingernails on a schoolroom blackboard.

What was the matter with the dumb turd? Anyone could see the ugly little dame didn't put out. And come to think of it, what was the matter with *her?* Anyone could see the guy was lusting for her drab flesh. Maybe she didn't have anything to read upstairs?

He checked his watch again. It couldn't be that early. Gaston had left sometime during the last ice age and Rome had fallen while he was getting that last drink from the bar.

A guest dressed like a Gibson Girl came in. She wore no hat, so he knew she'd come down from an upstairs room. He tried to ignore her. It wasn't easy. She was a stunning brunette with

cameo features and eyes so big he could tell they were blue,
even in this dim light.

It was safe to look her over as she stood at the bar with her
back to him, of course, so he did. He liked the view from that
angle, too. The waistline above the hip-hugging whipcord skirt
she wore had to be the result of a painfully tight corset.
Nobody hourglassed that nicely without expensive, impractical
underwear. Her outer duds were more sensible for the tropics,
though. The thin khaki blouse above the whipcord skirt looked
like she planned some jungle running. She obviously hadn't
already done any. Her pinned-up hair and ivory skin hadn't
spent much time down here yet. The last dame he'd had had
been a blond native. He'd had to knock her out before she'd
half-satisfied him. He wondered what it would be like to
switch to a dark-haired white woman. He decided he'd better
not try to find out.

The tall horsey guy and the ugly little sparrow crossed his
line of vision, arm in arm and obviously going somewhere in a
hurry. He repressed a chuckle. It just went to show that you
just couldn't judge a cunt by its cover. He got up and moved
his hat, his drink, and himself over to the corner they'd
vacated. He'd noticed it was a better place to wait for Gaston.
As he seated himself in one of the side-by-side leather chairs,
he saw that he now had both the side door and the lobby
entrance covered. He was less noticeable from the bar now.
The barkeep had to crane to see into this corner, and the dame
he was serving was now half-hidden by a pillar. The window
to his left opened onto the alley and gave him a sneaky preview
of anyone making for the side entrance. He saw the steam car
still parked out there. Otherwise the alley was empty and, as it
was blind, anyone coming up it would have his back to the
window unless he looked in obviously.

The brunette came back in view as she turned from the bar
and walked his way with a tall highball glass. He kept his eyes
polite. He could look her over some more when she sat down

some place with her profile to him. She came all the way to his corner, sat down in the chair the horsey guy had vacated, and said, "I say, this is a spot of luck, Captain Gringo! We'd about given up on you still being in town!"

He stared at her silently. Even up close, he knew he'd never seen her before. Hers was the kind of face a guy remembered, if he had any glands at all. She dimpled even prettier and continued, "It's all right. I'm on your side. We tried to recruit you in Costa Rica, but you and your little French friend were nowhere to be found in San José. I'm Sylvia Porter, by the way."

"So who is Sylvia?" he asked, smiling thinly. The accent was British. But their old chum Greystoke of British Intelligence wouldn't have been looking for them in Costa Rica. They'd just done a job for the prick up the coast, and been stiffed.

She said, "I'm with a syndicate of treasure hunters. We're on our way to Laguna Caratasca, just up the coast. It's supposed to be deserted these days. Just in case it's not, we picked up a couple of Maxim machine guns. They say you're the best machine gunner south of Texas. True?"

There was no sense being modest, since she already had his number. He shrugged and said, "Great minds sure run in the same channel. Gaston Verrier and I were thinking about Laguna Caratasca. We gave it up as too iffy."

She frowned and asked, "You already know about the pirate treasure? We thought it was our own little secret. But if it's already on the grapevine, we may need you more than ever."

He kept a card close to his vest by not saying he didn't know what the hell she was talking about. Instead, he asked, "How did you know I'd be here? I didn't know, myself, until a little while ago!"

She explained, "We heard you were in town. Half of Nicaragua seems to be looking for you, and not to *hire* you! Running into you here was sheer good fortune for both of us.

One of our party heard you'd run into the perishing jungle. That's where all the enthusiastic local law officers are right now, you'll be pleased to know."

She looked around thoughtfully, nodded, and added, "I might have known you'd run to earth in a place like this. Very neat. I'd never think to look for such a desperado in such sedate surroundings." Then she said, "But you can't last long on your own. Do you want the job with us?"

"Tell me about it."

She sipped her sweet rum highball and gathered her thoughts before she explained, "There are a dozen in my syndicate. All British, of course. These perishing natives would murder us for the gold if and when we find it. We have one English remittance man who says he can lead us to the lagoon. But he hasn't been there in several years and we have conflicting stories on Laguna Caratasca. Some say there's been nobody there since the Royal Navy cleaned it out a few years ago. Others say land pirates have moved in to replace the sea pirates who used to hunt out of there. What do you think, Captain Gringo?"

"Call me Dick; you're not a Mexican. I can't tell you anything about the area. I've never been there. Gaston has, ten years or so out of date. I can't see what bandits would be doing there. Who would they rob? The idea of Laguna Caratasca in the bad old days was that it was too far from the Honduran capital up in the highlands for Honduran law to care about. There are no towns there, officially. The lagoon's over fifty miles long on the map. The map shows the larger islands. Probably leaves off a mess of little turtle keys and reefs are up for grabs."

"We have a map. A treasure map at that. The Royal Navy didn't nail all the coast pirates. But, like your friend Gaston, our map is out of date. Hurricanes can play havoc with sandbars and mangrove swamps in ten or twelve years. But let's worry about that when we get there. You *did* say you were coming, didn't you?"

He didn't even have a hard-on. He said, "I'm thinking about it. What kind of a boat do you kiddies have? You're talking about shallow, treacherous waters on a lee coast. Do you have auxiliary power?"

She pointed her dimpled chin at the window beyond him and said, "We're driving motorcars, by *land*. My Stanley's right outside. The others are up the quay, near the north end of town."

He blinked in surprise and said, "You never *drove* from Costa Rica!"

She laughed and said, "Of course not. That's why most of our vehicles are still on the quay. We unloaded them the other day from a coastal steamer."

"For God's sake, why?"

"Don't you see how clever it is, Dick? Anyone watching for strangers at Laguna Caratasca will have all eyes, and hopefully all guns, trained on the seaward approaches. Our guide knows a jungle trail running from here in Nicaragua to the landward side of the big lagoon. In the bad old days, the pirates used it to carry loot and supplies across the border. One assumes they had some arrangement with the Nicaraguan government of the time. Before you object about that, the Nicaraguan Conservatives were in power and cahoots with the coast pirates. The law here, *now,* knows next to nothing."

He sighed and said, "Neither do you guys, if you think you can drive horseless carriages up the Mosquito Coast a good sixty miles! I hate to have to be the one to tell you this, doll, but you don't see many filling stations along your average jungle trail. Said trails were not hacked out with rubber tires in mind, either!"

She said, "Pooh! We knew that when we ordered steam cars instead of internal-combustion or electrics. The Stanley brothers build a very sturdy machine. There's water everywhere, and almost anything that will burn will keep said water boiling. Our steamers have been fitted with heavy-duty lorry springs and solid rubber tires."

"Ouch. Okay, it might work if you drive slow, and I don't see how anyone could drive fast through a jungle. Let's talk about the machine guns. How much ammo would I have if push came to shove?"

"We have a couple of cases for each gun."

"That's not enough. A Maxim spits six hundred rounds a minute if you're shooting at anyone important. If four cases of thirty-thirty will stop 'em, they ain't all that important."

"Brrr! You do paint a grim picture. If I can get you more ammo, will you take the job?"

"Where can you get a couple of thousand extra rounds, and, more important, what's in it for Gaston and me?"

"You mean *money?* Well, your share in the treasure would come to one-fourteenth, since there'd be fourteen of us, all told. Does that sound fair?"

"Hell no! I might have known you were asking us to work on spec! What if we don't find any treasure? Lots of old drunks sell maps, you know."

She sniffed and said, "I assure you we got the map from a good source, which I'm not at liberty to discuss. Try it another way. What happens if you stay here in Puerto Cabezas when we drive on?"

"You paint grim pictures, too. Okay. Gaston's not going to like it, but we'll see you safely to Laguna Caratasca and maybe hang around long enough to see if you look like you know what you're doing. If all we find up there are mosquitoes and snakes, all bets are off!"

She held out her hand to shake on it. Her hand felt nice in his as she said, "Good. We were planning to leave tonight, after the paseo ran down and the natives were less restless. I'd better drive up the quay and see about more ammo. There's a no-questions chandler up there who's already sold us supplies he asked us never to mention to his current government."

He hung on to her hand to keep her seated as he said, "Hold it. Half the natives here think horseless carriages run on black magic, and most of them are on the street right now!"

"Oh, you're right. I'd better pop into a hired horse-drawn hack. Do you want to tag along, Dick?"

"Want to. Can't. I promised to wait here for Gaston. How do I find you guys if things get confusing?"

"My friends are at another posada, called La Golondrina, next to the warehouse we have the other cars in. The chandler's shop is right down the quay and . . . Never mind; if you have to leave here in a hurry, go to the warehouse next to La Golondrina. I'll tell everyone to expect you."

She got her hand back and rose to leave before he could ask more. He had a couple of questions indeed. But if she was a police informant, she sure liked to do things the complicated way.

He got up and went to the bar for another drink. He'd been tipping well and the black barkeep had gotten friendlier every time he served him. So Captain Gringo said, "I forgot to ask the lady I was just with her room number. You, ah, wouldn't like to have a drink on me, would you?"

The barkeep smiled knowingly, but said, "I can't help you, señor. She is a stranger to me, too. She must have just checked in, like yourself."

The tall American nodded and took his drink back to the corner to brood a bit. But wait a minute. Sylvia's car had been parked out in the alley when they arrived. She couldn't have had them tailed from the whorehouse. So what was left?

He sipped his drink as he considered. He nodded and muttered half-aloud, "Sure. They know your rep and they knew the cops were breathing down your back. She came down to this end of town and parked while she had a discreet peek at the few places a smart-ass guy on the run might duck into. How many could there be in a town this size?"

He was a third of the way down the gin and tonic when Gaston popped in via the lobby entrance, spotted him, and came over as fast as he could walk without running. Gaston didn't sit down. He said, "Let's go. I think I spotted someone on my tail, just as I turned in to the front entrance!"

Captain Gringo put the glass on an end table and got up, saying, "Side exit. I've got something to tell you if we make it."

They strolled to the door through which they'd first entered. Captain Gringo put a casual hand on the knob and twisted. The door was locked. He looked thoughtfully at the barkeep, who seemed intent on wiping something awful off the mahogany and wasn't looking their way. Captain Gringo growled, "Know any other neat places to hole up? I might have known they'd have a telephone out in the fucking lobby!"

Gaston didn't answer. He'd whipped out his gun to blast the first cop coming through the archway from the lobby!

The uniformed intruder went down nicely, but there had to be more where he came from. Captain Gringo growled, "Shoot that barkeep!" as he picked up a potted palm, brass pot and all. He'd said it in English, so the barkeep was too slow in ducking and Gaston nailed him right over the left eye, as Captain Gringo threw the potted palm through the glass by the side of the treacherously locked door, pot and all.

He drew his own .38 as he dived out the opening. Behind him, Gaston put another cop on the lobby rug before diving out after him. They got as far as the parked Stanley Steamer before some other prick leaned around the corner at the far end of the alley and winged a shot at them before ducking back out of sight.

Gaston said, *"Merde alors,* we are boxed!"

But Captain Gringo said, "No, we're not. Get in that car. I'm driving, so cover me!"

Gaston hesitated a split second, grasped the idea, and leaped up on the high seat behind the low hood. Captain Gringo jumped in beside him, released the parking brake, and opened the steam throttle. The results scared even him.

The Stanley Steamer had its shortcomings. But he guessed nobody was going to build a faster automobile until well into the coming century. As the dry steam hit the powerful cylinders between the rear wheels, the big horseless carriage burned rubber all the way out of the alley and was doing at least fifty when it hit the street!

"Turn, *turn*, you maniac!" wailed Gaston as they tore straight at a storefront across the way, while bewildered bullets whipped through the spaces they kept leaving. Captain Gringo swung the wheel hard over and they slid broadside, solid tires screaming and smoking until they decided which way they wanted to go. And then, as the startled cops all around the posada hurled lead and curses, they were gone in a cloud of blue rubber smoke and kerosene fumes!

Captain Gringo swung inland at the next corner to tear blindly up the narrow dark street, while Gaston made more noise about it than the nearly silent steam engine. Captain Gringo said, "Yeah, yeah, I heard you," and swung around another corner before braking to a stop to get his bearings. He spotted the moon above the rooftops, nodded, and opened the throttle again, more sedately. As they purred quietly as a cat along the northbound back street, he said, "We could light the headlamps. But that would *really* attract attention. Doesn't this thing run neat, Gaston? Listen. It makes less noise than two giggly girls on bikes!"

Gaston crossed himself and said, "You just cost me a year's growth!" Then he laughed and added, "I think we just made some flicks wet their pants, too! Where are we going in this locomotive, my impetuous youth? I know this village lane from old. The pavement, such as it is, ends less than a mile away!"

"I know. Isn't it nice to have it all to ourselves with everyone in town flirting over at the main plaza? There must be a few old farts who stayed home tonight. But who's going to hear us from inside? Boy, this is some buggy. If it were a Duryea or even a Benz, we'd be making enough noise for a modest revolution between these stucco walls on either side. This thing makes no more noise than a kitten pissing under the sofa!"

"It's adorably discreet, Dick. Now tell me where the fuck we're *going* in it!"

So Captain Gringo filled him in on Sylvia Porter's offer as they cruised silently toward the warehouse where she'd said to meet her. Gaston heard him out before he snorted in disgust and said, *"Sacre bleu,* they sound like amateurs who just escaped from an English boarding school. Have you any idea how many old pirate treasure maps are circulating, Dick?"

"I told her some drunk had probably whipped it up on hotel stationery aged with coffee, Gaston. But look at the bright side. They have the money to buy toys like this steam car and those machine guns."

*"Oui,* but you said they expect us to join the party just for the pleasure of their company. I told you I passed through Laguna Caratasca when it was still a pirate base, Dick. If anyone in that *très* scruffy crew had enough treasure to see fit for burial, he never mentioned it to *me!"*

"Hey, what can I tell you? If you were a pirate, would you blab about your buried treasure to everyone just passing through? Besides, it doesn't matter what they're looking for up there. Even if her whole story is a crock of shit, Sylvia offered us a way out of here! Everyone else we've met went and called the law. And by the way, she's not bad-looking, either!"

•   •   •

Sylvia Porter was pretty as ever, but she seemed a bit chagrined when they drove in the back door of the warehouse and slid to a stop with a squeal of rubber, just inches from the side of a big black sedan made by White in the States. As the English girl and her companions stared at him in surprise, Captain Gringo called out, "Sorry. I'm not used to such sudden responses. You'd better get in back, Sylvia. We left the place you parked it with lots of guns going off. Did you get the ammo, and where are the Maxims?"

Before she could answer, a big husky guy with a toothbrush mustache shouted, "Who in God's name are these blokes, Sylvia?"

Captain Gringo let her explain as he looked over the rest of the expedition. There were four steam cars lined up in the warehouse, making it five vehicles for fourteen people. Not bad, even with all the shit they had piled in or strapped on the big heavy horseless carriages.

There were three other women in addition to Sylvia. They, like the men, wore light tan travel dusters. The eight male members of Sylvia's crew interested him even less. All but one. He nodded at the stubby guy who'd been reading the paper so much in Madam Fifi's and said, "So now we know how you guys found us. You've all been busy little bees. Now it's time we all buzzed off. Which of you is the guide Sylvia said we were supposed to have?"

The stubby guy he'd taken for a possible police informant smiled sheepishly and said, "That's me, Captain Gringo. I was trying to find a moment alone with you at Madam Fifi's, but you seemed, ah, otherwise occupied. When the police arrived, I naturally gave up on waiting for you two to come back down. How in the devil did you chaps get out of there? They had the perishing block surrounded!"

"We flew with the pigeons. Do you have a name?"

"Oh, sorry, Marlowe, here. Alfred Marlowe, late of Essex and all that."

"Okay, Al. You can call me Dick. You know Gaston's handle. Like I said, it's time to get out of here. So why don't you get the lead out and take the damned point?"

Marlowe looked uncertainly at the one with the toothbrush on his upper lip and asked, "Major Wallace?"

The husky Wallace frowned at Captain Gringo and asked, "Are you sure you were followed? We hadn't planned to leave just yet."

"They don't have to follow anyone to figure out, sooner or later, that if you're looking for a horseless carriage, you go to the only place in town where they *are!* You guys didn't unload these steam cars hidden under your dusters, for God's sake! Sylvia told me the plan to leave at a more discreet hour. It was a swell idea, but I just blew it. If we don't leave now, forget it!"

Major Wallace didn't look like he was used to taking suggestions from other people. But he nodded stiffly and said, "Very well. Everyone mount up as we planned. You take the lead, Marlowe. No headlamps, of course, until we're well clear of this perishing village!"

There was a mad scramble as everyone piled aboard the vehicles they'd been practicing with. Sylvia and another girl came to the steam car Captain Gringo and Gaston were in. She said, "You two had best sit in the back. I'm driving."

"I know how to drive this thing, Sylvia."

"That's what I mean, Dick. Move out of the way, dammit! Marlowe's already starting and we have no tail lamps to follow!"

Captain Gringo and Gaston rolled over the back of the front seat to make room for the two girls. The one now seated by Sylvia was named Pat. It was hard to see what she looked like. The light was dim and Pat wore a big hat with a mosquito veil as well as her shapeless duster.

Sylvia let the major's vehicle follow Marlowe's out the wide rear doors of the warehouse before she fed the Stanley some steam and followed smoothly and silently. Gaston chuckled and said, "Now this, Dick, is how I was just trying to tell you one should drive a horseless carriage!"

Captain Gringo ignored the jibe and asked Sylvia again about the machine guns. She said, "In the major's car, just ahead. Those pine crates in the backseat. We can worry about them when we need them."

He looked back, saw nothing but the dim outlines of the steam cars behind, and muttered, "When we *need* them, she says! We're maybe a hop and two skips ahead of the cops, and the only serious weapons on hand are not on hand. When's the last time those Maxims were stripped and cleaned, Sylvia?"

"Cleaned and stripped? Whatever for? They're still in the packing they came in from the factory. Major Wallace said we should wait till we had someone who knew something about machine guns before we unpacked them."

The two soldiers of fortune exchanged glances. Captain Gringo saw no need to explain to anyone that dumb. Gaston snorted in disgust and said, *"Eh bien,* the humidity is only about ninety down here at this time of the year. Perhaps *all* the grease did not run off as the adorable weapons sweltered in their soggy wooden crates, *non?"*

Captain Gringo didn't answer. When he had a chance to open the crates, he'd see if they had two weapons that would shoot, enough sound parts to cannibalize into one that might, or a lot of expensive rust that wouldn't shoot at all. He asked Sylvia again if they had the extra ammo. She hadn't answered the first time he'd asked. She nodded and said, "It's in the last automobile. The White you almost demolished coming in."

Gaston said, "Oh, I love it. The Maxims are up ahead, the ammunition is trailing well to the rear, and the only ones who can man a machine gun are driving through the countryside with pretty girls all in a row."

He looked off into the darkness and added, "Speaking of countryside, where in the devil are we? There used to be a moon around here somewhere. I can't see a thing!"

Sylvia, at the wheel, answered calmly, "I can feel the ruts we're following. Don't worry, Gaston. If Marlowe steers into a tree, we'll hear it in plenty of time."

"I think I'd rather get out and walk," Gaston said with a sigh.

Captain Gringo had to admit that he had a point. They weren't going fast. About six miles an hour, as far as he could judge as he spotted an occasional lighter blur they passed in the darkness. But he said, "We're moving faster than any troops can march. We don't have to stop for trail breaks, either. Do you know if the law back there has horses, Gaston?"

Gaston shook his head and said, "Not the town constabulary. The military of course has cavalry. But it should take them a day or so to get over to this coast. Why, did you want to steal a *horse*, too?"

"No, just figuring the odds. If Marlowe doesn't run us into a swamp before morning, we'll make it to the border by daybreak at the rate we're moving. The Nicaraguans can figure that out as well as we can, so they probably won't chase us seriously."

"Ah, in that case, may I suggest we all slow down, m'mselle? I believe you about solid rubber tires. My kidneys will never forgive you, even at this modest speed."

Sylvia said, "I know the road's bumpy. I'm the one who's trying to keep us in the ruts. We have to keep up with the lead automobiles and Marlowe seems to be a speed demon."

They hit a bump that would have flipped them had they been going fifteen miles an hour. Pat gleeped in terror and would have fallen out had not Gaston reached forward to grab her as Captain Gringo cursed and Sylvia called her steering wheel something worse. He said, "Jesus, he must be in a hurry. You say Marlowe's the guy who knows the old coastal pirate layout. I hope you kiddies didn't buy the map from him."

"Heavens, no. I told you he was a remittance man. Major Wallace found him a couple of weeks ago, down the coast. He speaks like a man from a good family. They obviously sent him over here to keep him from disgracing them. He's all right when he's sober and, thanks to the major, he usually is, these days."

"I know what a remittance man is. American families have black sheep too. What was Marlowe doing up the coast in the bad old days? He doesn't look like a pirate."

"I doubt he has the backbone to steal fruit off a stand. He wasn't there with any pirates. I told you the Royal Navy cleaned them out long ago, back in the days when you Yanks weren't so fussy about your silly Monroe Doctrine and Great Britain almost claimed this whole area. You know of course that the Royal Navy still uses Bluefields, down the other way, even though your tiresome President Cleveland keeps insisting it belongs to Nicaragua?"

"Never mind about the Monroe Doctrine. Just get us out of Nicaragua. Did Marlowe say what he was doing up in Laguna Caratasca if it was after the pirates had been cleaned out?"

Pat said, "I heard him tell the major he was with some turtle hunters. Apparently there's a lot of turtle grass on the tidal flats of the big lagoon."

Captain Gringo nudged Gaston and asked, "Pearls?"

Gaston shook his head and said, *"Mais non.* He was probably really there with turtle hunters. There are no pearl beds in such shallow stagnant water. As I recall from my previous romp through the swampy place, turtles make more sense than anything else. Piracy is no longer allowed, and there is no great profit in mosquito skins, even though the ones up there are big enough to skin."

Pat laughed and said, "Surely you jest? No insects could possibly be that big!"

Captain Gringo had learned at his mother's knee never to play cards with strangers on a train or attempt to explain a joke to a Brit. But Gaston had enjoyed hauling Pat back from the brink a

few times by now, so he said soberly, "You have not been in
the tropics long, I see. When I was an artillery officer in the
Mexican army, we found, after wearing out many a mule, that
nothing pulled field guns as well as the local cockroaches.
They are harder to break to harness than mules, of course. But
once one has them properly trained . . ."

"Oh, you're pulling my leg!" Pat giggled, adding, "I've
seen the great roaches down here. I nearly fainted the first time
one ran across my poor foot. But they're not much bigger than
mice, or maybe rats."

"True. We used to hitch them to our field guns in
twenty-roach teams. As to pulling your leg, which one would
you prefer I start with, M'mselle?"

The silly conversation ended when Sylvia responded to a
beep up ahead by braking hard. The two men in the back
almost fell atop the girls in front as the steam car slid to a stop.
Captain Gringo asked what was up. Sylvia said, "I don't
know. We haven't driven far enough to need fresh boiler
water."

Captain Gringo thought about that as the tiny gleam of a
bull's-eye lantern slowly came their way in the darkness all
around. In his earlier enthusiasm for the Stanley Steamer he'd
forgotten why the electric and internal-combustion jobs were
still giving steam cars a run for the money.

Already heavy to start with, steam cars saved weight by
having no condensers. Like railroad locomotives, they used
the steam once and had to drink more boiler water from time to
time. Unlike railroad locomotives, they only had little boilers
that could fit under a horseless carriage hood. So they had to
stop for water more often.

He stood up in the high-riding Stanley and looked back.
Nothing. The drivers behind had stopped, thank God. If
anyone was following them up the coast road, they were as
much in the dark as he was. But they couldn't be far from
Puerto Cabezas yet.

The guy with the little spotlight turned out to be Major Wallace. He shone the light on Sylvia and said, "We may as well take this opportunity to top our boiler water. That beggar Marlowe seems to have lost his bloody way!"

Sylvia replied, "For heaven's sake, we can't be fifteen miles out of town yet!"

"That's what I mean!" sighed Wallace, sweeping his beam off to the side at the banana trees all around as he added, "We're still in settled country and Marlowe's balked at the first damned fork in the road we've come to!"

Captain Gringo said, "Hold it, major. Swing that light a little to your left and, yeah, hold it there. Do you see what I see, Gaston?"

Gaston was already climbing down as Wallace ran his beam up and down the bare wooden pole, saying, "It's a telegraph pole. What of it?"

Captain Gringo said, "Gaston will get the wire. He climbs like a squirrel. It's a habit we've picked up, with all sorts of nasty people chasing us."

Gaston moved into the beam, making for the pole, as Wallace said, "We'd better not. It may give our position away, and by now they should have wired ahead, if that was the plan."

Captain Gringo said, "If they don't know we took this road out of town, the whole town's blind. They may already have wired up the coast. They may not have thought of it yet. First we make sure they *can't*. Then we make sure we don't drive into any village with telegraph poles leading into it!"

Wallace shrugged and said, "Well, we hired you as security. I have to tell the others to top their boilers."

He moved on in the dark. Sylvia had climbed down and, as far as Captain Gringo could tell in the dark, was handling something metallic. He climbed down too, asking, "Where are you and how can I help, doll?"

She said, "Stay out of my blinking way if you don't like being scalded. I have the water canister, and I can find my way to the bathroom in the dark, thank you very much."

Captain Gringo took a cigar from his breast pocket to kill two birds with one stone when he struck a match. By the flickering little light he could see Sylvia pouring water into a little tank under the now open hood. The feed tank was fastened to the firewall ahead of the steering wheel. Most of the space under the hood was occupied by a modest-sized boiler wrapped in piano wire. No light escaped from the oil-fired firebox under it. He asked, "Don't you think we might as well feed her some more kerosene while we're at it? I drove this thing a ways before we found you guys, you know."

She said, "You damned near burned the tires off doing it, too. And *we* are not tending this vehicle. *I* am tending this blinking vehicle. The fuel's not the problem. The dial on the dash tells me we've more than enough kerosene in the tank under my seat. Before you ask, yes, we do have extra tins of fuel and water in the rear trunk."

He didn't see what she had to bitch about. He shook out the match and walked up to Major Wallace's car ahead. He hauled one of the crates over the rear, dropped it to the roadway, and used his pocketknife to open the lid. He struck another light. The Maxim machine gun lay in a bed of wood chips, and as he gagged at the vile smell of castor oil he saw it was in pretty good shape, save for rust spots here and there where the oil had been absorbed by the packing. He left the tripod in the case as he pulled the Maxim into an upright position, took a kerchief from his pocket, and wiped it down until it was clean enough to carry. Then he picked it up and took it back to the other vehicle. Sylvia had finished topping her boiler and asked what smelled so awful. He put the machine gun in the back and replied, "I like to keep busy. They packed the machine guns in castor oil, bless their hearts. These are secondhand black-market guns, right?"

"I don't know. You'll have to ask the major."

He shrugged, went back to reload the crate into the major's vehicle, then moved down the line to get some ammo. He encountered the Englishman with the bull's-eye, which came as no great surprise. Wallace said, "Oh, it's you. What are you doing out of your seat? We have to get a move on."

Captain Gringo said, "No, we don't. Your guide is lost. I'll talk to you about that in a minute. Got to get some ammo."

"Whatever for? Have you seen or heard something, Walker?"

"Not yet. I want a belt in the Maxim when and if I *do!* Hold your horseless carriages till Gaston gets down off that pole. Marlowe's not the only guy around here who knows his way to Laguna Caratasca."

"Oh, I say! That does solve the problem! I'll put him up in Marlowe's White Steamer and . . ."

"No, you won't. Gaston and me are a team. Let me get the ammo. Then we'll take the lead with Pat and Sylvia. As you move up the line, pass the word to light the headlights."

"Are you mad? What if someone spots our lights?"

"I'll be sitting above Sylvia with a loaded machine gun. Gaston only moves like a cat. He can't really *see* in the dark."

He saw that wasn't going down too well with the self-important Wallace, so he added soothingly, "Look, we're clear of the town, and the cops don't seem to be chasing us. They must have figured out how futile it is to chase horseless carriages on foot."

"Yes, but if they wired ahead . . ."

"That's why we'd better drive faster and have some idea what the front bumper's aimed at. I know our headlights will be spotted by anyone setting up a roadblock. But so what? *We* want to see *them,* too! These steam cars are pretty quiet, but not that quiet. Guys crouched behind a log across the road would hear us coming and open up before we knew they were there in any case, see?"

Wallace hesitated, then said, "Well, they say you know your business," and moved on before Captain Gringo could think of a polite way to ask just who *they* might be.

He was still thinking about that as he groped his way to the last vehicle, told the people in it what he wanted, and was handed a bulky square canister. He told the driver about the change in plans, adding, "Don't turn on your headlights until you hear a beep from the head of the column. Do any of you guys have a gun?"

One of the men in the back said he was holding a Winchester across his knees. Captain Gringo said, "Don't hold it across your knees. Prop it over the back of your seat and keep your eyes to the rear. You guys are tail end. So anyone on our tail will nail you first if you don't spot *him* first."

Having cheered them immensely, Captain Gringo returned to his own steam car to find Gaston already in the rear seat. He handed the ammo to the Frenchman and climbed in behind the two girls before he told Sylvia about the change in plans, adding, "It could get a little rough up at the head of this motorcade. Maybe you girls should ride with the major?"

"Who would drive?" asked Sylvia, adding, "No. I've seen the way *you* drive."

Pat said, "The other vehicles are crowded. Aside from passengers, the gear we were supposed to have strapped to this steamer had to be tossed in the others willy-nilly when we left so suddenly."

There went the chance he wanted to consult with Gaston privately. He nodded and said, "Okay, switch on your headlights and see if we can move up between the bananas and the cars ahead."

Sylvia did no such thing. She climbed out again, walked around to the front of the Stanley, and lit the headlights with a match. As she got back in, he frowned and asked, "Isn't there any way to dim those lights from behind the wheel?"

"How? Only the electric cars have Edison bulb headlights. Ours run on carbide."

She fed steam and they lurched out of the ruts to bounce over the weeds until they'd passed Wallace's and Marlowe's steamers. As she stopped just ahead of the original lead vehicle, they saw why Marlowe had stopped. The road ahead forked at a thirty-degree angle. Sylvia stopped, too. Captain

Gringo said, "Beep your beeper. I didn't know it took so long to light up. Gaston?"

Gaston waited till Sylvia squeezed the bulb of the horn mounted by her side before he said, "We take the fork to the left, m'mselle."

"Are you sure?" she asked, adding, "The road that way is almost overgrown with weeds, and besides, it leads inland. I thought we were trying to follow the coast line."

Gaston said, "We are. A very *soggy* coast line, m'mselle. The fork to the right is heavily traveled and doubtless leads to some plantation on one of the coves the Mosquito Coast is so tediously provided with. We want to go the shorter, hopefully drier way on the higher ground to the west."

Captain Gringo looked back, saw that the other four cars were lit up, and told Sylvia, "Take the left fork. He only lies about bugs and his sex life." So Sylvia shrugged, fed steam, and followed the route Gaston had picked. The solid rubber wheels rolled more softly in the weed-filled ruts of the overgrown wagon trace. Captain Gringo didn't have to suggest speeding up a bit. Sylvia knew what she was doing. He hauled the machine gun into his lap and began to field strip it by feel, putting the parts in the side pocket of his jacket as he made sure they were all there. The castor oil was going to stink him up like a skunk with an overprotective mother, but it couldn't be helped, and while castor oil was an awful thing to make a kid swallow, it couldn't be beat as a lubricant in humid heat. Lots of racing drivers used it in their red-hot engines since it burned off without leaving charred carbon on the metal. He checked the bore with a match when Sylvia slowed for a water-filled dip. The gun seemed in good shape. He adjusted the head spacing, since it had apparently been fired hot by the previous owner. There was no water in the jacket, of course. Captain Gringo didn't water a Maxim unless he meant to fire long serious bursts, and there wasn't that much ammo to spare, even with the extra rounds he'd asked for. He started putting the gun back together as he told Gaston they were in business, and asked the Frenchman to hand him the end of an ammo belt. Gaston did so, saying, "I find it *très* curious about your M'sieur Marlowe getting lost back there, don't you, Dick?"

"What can I tell you? He must have needed the job. At least he can drive, even if he fibbed about knowing the way to Laguna Caratasca."

"*Merde alors*, even a beachcomber should have been able to read that fork in the road back there!"

"So he's not a good beachcomber. I read it the same way, and I've never been anywhere near the lagoon."

Pat turned brightly in her seat to say, "Oh, I understand why we went this way! If the pirates and everyone else no longer use this road, it accounts for the weeds, right?"

One could see her profile under the veil now, with the glow ahead outlining her. Pat didn't look as dumb as she sounded. She was sort of pretty in a pug-nosed way. Gaston said, "Bless you, my child. Stick with me and I'll smother you in rhinestones. You have the makings of a beachcomber, but this wagon trace has not been completely abandoned for ten or more years. Unless wheels roll from time to time, what they so amusingly describe as weeds in these parts soon grow up to be trees."

Pat just frowned in concentration. Sylvia got it. She said, "Then we still may run into traffic on this effing road?"

Captain Gringo said, "Not at night. Guys driving an ox cart of bananas to town like to have more light on the subject."

The headlights picked up something black and shiny slithering off the ruts ahead, so he added, "See what I mean?"

"My God, was that a snake?"

"Yeah, don't ask me what kind. They come in all varieties down here and most of them hunt just after sundown. By midnight most of the snakes and people down here call it a night."

Gaston slapped the side of his face, swore, and said, "The mosquitoes don't. I got the monster just as she was about to fly off to her nest with me. Could you drive a little faster, m'mselle? Dick and I are not wearing veils, and the night-flying bloodsuckers will get worse before they get better!"

Morning found the motorcade surrounded by what they hoped was uninhabited jungle. Mist hugged the ground between the mossy boles of glandular trees on either side. It was even mistier out on the silent sheet of water ahead. The weedy ruts they'd followed through the night ended in the fetid mud of a riverbank. As Sylvia braked to a stop, she asked, "Is that the Rio Segovia, Gaston?"

He said, *"Oui,* and I am feeling rather smug about it. I was beginning to wonder why we didn't seem to be getting to it. As I said, it was a long time ago."

Captain Gringo started to ask how far north they'd come from Puerto Cabezas. Then he remembered that the border was sixty miles as the crow flies. They hadn't been riding crows. The goddamn road had twisted all over as it followed the high ground. But he had to admit they'd never have made such good time on foot, or even mounted. Anyone chasing them was out of the race. Assuming, of course, they kept moving. Unless steam cars floated, that was going to be a problem.

He turned to Gaston and asked, "Okay, you're the world traveler. How does one find a ferry boat around here on such short notice?"

Gaston said, "You don't need one. The Segovia is shallow enough to ford here. Why else did you think the trail led here?"

The American studied the wide sheet of sluggish tea-colored water as Sylvia asked how deep it was. Gaston said, "It comes up to one's chest as one wades across, crocodiles permitting."

Captain Gringo had been afraid he'd say something like

that. The tops of the steam cars would make it. Their low-slung fire boxes wouldn't.

The others of course had also stopped. Major Wallace came forward with the shame-faced Marlowe. Wallace said, "I say, you told me there was a bridge, Marlowe!"

Marlowe looked down and muttered, "I told you last night this wasn't the trail I remembered. I came down the coast by another."

Wallace grimaced and turned to Captain Gringo to observe, "At least there seems to be no military outpost guarding the border, eh what?"

Captain Gringo repressed a snort of disgust and said, "I admire a man who thinks ahead. I could have told you there'd be no border guards. You only guard roads crossing your border when they *lead* someplace. According to Gaston here, there's no road up the coast beyond the lagoon country. So if Nicaragua's worried about being invaded by Honduras, or vice versa, this ain't the way either army would come. Smugglers always buy off the cops at both ends, so why bother about that either, see?" He turned to Gaston and said, "You and I had better scout the far side while the major here builds a lot of nice rafts. The sound of falling timber carries and we wouldn't want to be ambushed in the middle of a river, would we?"

Wallace asked, "Rafts?" Then, since nobody could really be that stupid, he added, "Oh, right, I'll have the chaps break out some saws and axes from the supplies."

Sylvia had been thinking. She said, "Wait a mo', you lot. Gaston says the water's only up to his chest. If I stand behind the wheel I won't even get my Aunt Fanny Adams wet."

Captain Gringo said, "You'll drown your fire, though."

She nodded and said, "I know. Not to worry. If we turn up the flames with the throttles shut and build up pressure till the safety valves are ready to pop, we can make it across with the fires out before the steam's all gone!"

Wallace laughed and said, "I say, the lass is on to something there! The river's not that wide. But tell me, Sylvia, won't we have to dry our burners a bit after drowning the poor things in that mucky brew?"

She shrugged and said, "We will. But meanwhile we'll be on the other side."

Captain Gringo climbed down, picked up the machine gun, and said, "You kiddies work it out. Meanwhile, we'll make sure there's nothing else to worry about on the far side. Gaston, grab the end of this belt. I don't want to get the canvas wet."

Gaston sighed and followed, holding the end of the ammo belt as he told Wallace, "Wait for our signal before you do anything grotesque. If you get no signal, forget about crossing. You children don't really wish to meet anything that can take the two of *us* out!"

Captain Gringo was already wading into the river, so Gaston had no choice but to follow, holding the ammo belt taut at shoulder height. Captain Gringo rested the Maxim on one shoulder to draw his .38 with the other hand as the bouillon-warm water rose around his thighs. Gaston murmured, "About those crocodiles I mentioned, Dick . . ."

But the taller American said, "Screw the crocodiles. There's nothing we can do about them. Keep your eyes on those fucking trees on the far shore. If you were out to ambush a motorcade you knew was coming your way, could you come up with a better place?"

"As a matter of fact, there are endless opportunities for ambush between here and the old pirate camp. But your point is well taken. Where did you suppose that telegraph wire I cut last night led to, Dick?"

"Not this way. I've been watching for wires."

The water rose higher until Gaston was in to the nipples and Captain Gringo was wet to the floating ribs. Then the slick muddy bottom started getting shallower again. They pressed on and floundered up the far bank. Said bank was low. The problem was the road beyond. There didn't seem to be any. Captain Gringo found a fallen log to brace the Maxim across as he growled, "Now I see why nobody was waiting for us on this side. Where's the fucking trail, Gaston?"

Gaston dropped the end of the ammo belt on the reasonably dry leaves as he looked around to get his bearings. Then he nodded and said, "Ah, there she is, the poor thing. As I observed last night just before the mosquitoes consumed me, when one does not use a jungle trail, it tries to heal itself. Those gumbo limbos are of recent vintage, Dick."

Captain Gringo spotted the ruts leading through the skinny saplings Gaston meant. Some of the young trees grew right in the ruts. He grunted and said, "Okay, when the Royal Navy cleans out a pirate cove it stays cleaned out. I'll cover the landward approaches with the Maxim just in case while you wave them on across. Okay?"

"Are you serious? You and I could doubtless follow the overgrown trail on foot, if we had machetes, but . . ."

"Wave them over, dammit! You don't need machetes if you've got a steel bumper and plenty of power. It's broad daylight and Sylvia's good at following ruts, so what the hell."

He moved back to the machine gun, muttering about having to do all the thinking around here. That was something to think about as he crouched down and fed a round into the chamber, pocketing the unfired round he'd spent to check the action again. There was something fishy as hell about the people they were traveling with these days.

He was having enough trouble buying the yarn about buried treasure. The coastal pirates who'd hung on long after the golden days of guys like Morgan and Rogers had been little more than half-breed scum, putting out to sea in sailing caribs to attack small coastal schooners. People with serious cargoes sent them by steamer these days. Nobody could board a steamship from a low-slung native craft. So how much treasure could the desperate riffraff have collected before the Royal Navy dealt with them as a general nuisance?

And even if Wallace and the others believed in pirate treasure, why were they going about recovering it in such a wrong-headed way? The steam cars and other expensive gear meant money, lots of money, behind this dumb operation. So why was it so dumb? Who'd ever heard of taking dames and other halfwits along if, as Wallace suspected, there could be an opposing team up at Laguna Caratasca.

The way most knock-around guys would have done it would have been a lot less complicated. He knew if it had been up to him, and he'd thought there was any point in going, he'd load up a lot of guns and hardcase guys aboard a power launch and just steam in the easy way. If there was an outfit strong enough to hold that big lagoon against a well-armed waterbone gang of pros, he wouldn't go.

He heard splashing. He glanced over his shoulder and saw Sylvia driving across, standing like a chariotress behind the wheel as she made like a steamboat with her steam car. He turned back to watch the trees. He'd worry about treachery from those quarters later. Whatever the weird Brits were up to, turning him and Gaston in for the rewards couldn't be it.

You don't drag wanted men across borders into uninhabited country to turn them in to the cops. Sylvia had spotted him at the hotel before he'd known who she was. So far, everything that she'd said was going to happen, had. He'd worry about her lying to him when he caught her in a lie. So far, she and her chums had just been acting terribly odd. Maybe the trouble Yanks had telling Brits a joke cut two ways. He sure didn't get the point of *this* joke, but he didn't see what else to call it!

Sylvia didn't think it was funny when she churned up the bank and saw Gaston waving her into the solid-looking wall of gumbo limbo, but she caught on fast and plowed into them, following the ruts by feel as Pat screamed and saplings went down like wheat, with the Stanley's bumper acting as the scythe. Sylvia drove a good fifty yards into the new growth before her pressure gave out and she had to stop.

The others came over in good order, save for Marlowe, who managed to stall in mid-stream. Major Wallace walked over to Captain Gringo, cursing, as the last car in the motorcade hissed to a soggy stop nearby. Wallace said, "Look at the perishing sod! He's waving at us like a ruddy shipwrecked sailor on a raft!"

Captain Gringo got to his feet, saying, "There doesn't seem to be anything to worry about over here. Keep your eyes skinned anyway. Mosquito Indian kids are liable to put an arrow into anything they stumble over just for the hell of it. I take it we've lost that White Steamer?"

"Not bloody likely. We can winch it out as soon as my firebox is dry. I had my steam car fitted with a winch geared to its engine, with just such emergencies in mind."

"Yeah, I can see you thought of everything. You sure picked a swell guide, major."

"*He* picked *me*, actually. As you know, we tried to recruit you or some chaps like you when we first arrived. You weren't in San José and we had no luck finding anyone else with your reputation. Marlowe approached us and said he heard we were mounting an expedition, so . . ."

"Gotcha. If you can't hire a pro, find a guy who needs drinking money. He got lost before we were barely clear of town last night. He's full of shit about having taken another road the last time. Gaston says this is the only one, and Gaston was making a living knowing things like that before you and I were born."

Wallace nodded and said, "I said he was a bloody sod. He just managed to mire his wheels out there, and I must say that took ingenuity, even for a moron! There's no way to stall a steam car if you have a full head of steam, damn his drunken soul!"

Captain Gringo saw Sylvia and Pat doing something under the hood of their Stanley. He moved over to join them, as Wallace strode up and down the bank, yelling out across the water for Marlowe either to wade ashore or, preferably, to drown himself.

Gaston came over too, as Sylvia slid the burner pan out to let the asbestos kerosene wicks have some air. Captain Gringo saw why Gaston was so interested in engineering these days. Both girls had removed their hats and veils, since the mosquitoes had been replaced by humid heat in the shade. Pat was a roguish-looking little Irish redhead with big green bedroom eyes, and the little Frenchman had dibs on her, damn his horny old soul!

Sylvia looked prettier, albeit more reserved, even with that grease on her pale cheek. He looked up at the sparkling green forest canopy and told them, "You'd better keep your lids on, ladies. It's not the sunlight you *see* that does you in in the tropics. The bigger trees have almost locked arms over this overgrown trail, but almost isn't good enough and some rays are getting through."

Sylvia said, "In a minute. The air's so perishing damp it's going to take forever for the burner to dry. Are we going to have to knock down trees all the way to Laguna Caratasca, for heaven's sake?"

"If we're lucky. The map says we have less than thirty miles to go. God knows what the jungle says." He turned to Gaston to ask, "Does the road ahead beeline or make like a snake, Gaston?"

Gaston snorted and said, "What road? M'mselle is correct in assuming it to be a rhubarb patch, these days. Most naturally it has always wound its weary way *très fatigue*. I think we'd do as well driving cross-country between the trees, *non?*"

Captain Gringo thought about that. He'd run through enough jungle by now to know it was true that the going was easier in the cathedral gloom of tall timber where sunlight never reached the ground to drive the underbrush crazy. He frowned and said, "Guys can walk pretty good between the big timber's buttress roots under virgin canopy. I'm not sure there's room to squeeze a motor vehicle through. You get to step over lots of fallen logs in the tall timber, too. Besides, how the hell could you ever find the way if we leave the only trail there?"

Gaston pointed to the gumbo limbo leaning away from Sylvia's front bumper and said, "Easy. This adorable hedgerow that used to be the trail should be headed the same way it always has, *non?*"

The taller American nodded thoughtfully and said, "It might work, if we kept a bearing on this wall of greenery as we drove. So which side do you suggest, east or west?"

"West, of course. One wishes to stay on the dry side."

Pat asked, "Coo, do you call this *dry?* I feel like I walked into a steambath with all my clothes on!"

Gaston suggested she take them off, adding, "We shall be wetter long before we are drier, even if it fails to rain today, M'mselle Pat. This trail followed such high ground as there was between here and the lagoons to the north. Fortunately, our high wheels should do most of the wading in the muck I foresee ahead."

Sylvia took Captain Gringo's elbow and steered him away from Gaston and the giggling little redhead. As they walked toward the river's edge, he thought she wanted to watch Major Wallace do something about the steam car still stuck out in the middle. But she avoided the pacing and cursing Wallace, too, as she murmured, "Dick, we have to do something about your friend Gaston."

"Really? I thought Pat had her eye on Gaston."

"That's what I'm talking about, and it's not bloody funny. He seems intent to have his way with her."

"I noticed. So what? Is she under twenty-one?"

"Mentally? I'd say she has the mind of a nine-year-old. One who'd just love to play doctor in the shed with the lad next door."

He chuckled and said, "Yeah, and I let Gaston get in the first bids. I guess you're not interested in playing doctor, huh?"

"Don't be beastly. How are we to keep that dirty old man out of poor Pat's knickers?"

"Are you her mother? Dirty old men need love and affection, too, and Pat can decide for herself about her knickers. He won't attack her, if that's what you're worried about."

Sylvia grimaced and said, "He won't have to. I noticed coming over on the ship that she can't say no. Had a dreadful row with her when she tried to bring a second-class passenger to the cabin I was forced to share with her."

"I see you don't like parties, either. Don't worry, Sylvia. Old Gaston is too sneaky to do anything naughty in front of you, unless you ask him. He's not a kiss-and-tell guy, if you're worried about the other guys getting jealous. By the way, I've been meaning to ask how you four dames and eight guys pair off."

"We don't," she said flatly, adding, "I told you in the beginning this was strictly a business syndicate. All of us but Marlowe, of course, knew Major Wallace socially in Blighty. When he approached us with the story of the treasure, each of us chipped in to mount this expedition. I confess my own interest was as much for the adventure as anything. I already have sufficient income for my needs, but, God, it can get dull in Belgravia if one's not interested in musical beds or an early grave from drugs and drink!"

He nodded as a couple of pieces fell into place. Belgravia, he knew, was a pretty fancy London neighborhood. He'd thought they all seemed sort of hoity-toity for a knock-around crew. It explained the dames tagging along, too. A bored rich dame who invested in a treasure hunt wasn't about to sit home with her sewing as she waited for results. It was still a hell of a way to run a railroad. He asked, "Is there any chance you kiddies could have been led down the garden path? Treasure hunts are a pretty standard con, you know."

"Don't be ridiculous. Major Wallace rowed for Harrow. Besides, he was a great friend of my late husband and . . ."

"You're a recent widow, Sylvia?" he cut in.

She shrugged and said, "Bruce died about two years ago. That's recent enough, if you're asking if I've another bloke in Blighty."

He didn't ask. He could tell by her occasional lapses into East End slang that she'd married up a couple of notches. That explained a few things, too. Even a nice Cockney widow with the wherewithal to go on living in Belgravia wouldn't make many friends of her own there. Major Wallace accepted people socially if they had the dough to back his whatever the hell. It was possible he really thought they were hunting for a long-lost treasure. There didn't seem to be anything more interesting up the coast.

One of the other male drivers and two of the remaining women in the party came over to join them. Captain Gringo couldn't remember their names and Sylvia didn't see fit to reintroduce them. The dames were both okay, although Sylvia and Pat were the prettier members of the pack. One of the other English girls wore glasses and spoke so veddy-veddy he could barely understand her as she asked how long they would be staying here. Captain Gringo pointed at the stalled steam car in the river and explained they had to wait until Wallace had power to winch Marlowe ashore. She said, "Oh, good. In that case I have time to take a shit," and strode grandly out of sight into the trees as Captain Gringo tried not to laugh. He knew she'd been born with *her* money. People raised by servants who always told them they were right didn't have to bother with learning middle-class manners.

The other man said, "I never would have hired that remittance man. Had to drive around him when he stalled out there. That Marlowe's a rum chap, even for a beachcomber. He lies, you see."

"Oh? I hadn't noticed."

The other man nodded soberly and said, "Marlowe claims to come from a good family in Essex. It so happens I have relations in Colchester."

"That'd be the county seat of Essex, right?"

The other man turned to the remaining other woman and said, "You see, Phoebe? Even a Yank knows his English geography better than that rum Marlowe beggar! The blighter tried to tell me his home was in Norwich, in Essex, of all bleeding shires!"

Captain Gringo envisioned his old geography atlas. It had been a long time since things like that had seemed important, but even he knew that Norwich was either in Connecticut or somewhere on the east coast of England. He shrugged and said, "Maybe he just didn't want to tell you where he really comes from. Family skeletons and all that."

"That's no flaming excuse to put Norwich, the cathedral town of Norfolk, in flaming Essex, two flaming shires to the south!"

The girl with him soothed, "Now, Bertie, don't be unkind. Mr. Marlowe's been away from England a long time and I'm sure Captain Walker's right about him wanting to hide some sticky family business."

"Then why can't he do it right, for God's sake? A bloody *Welshm*an would know where Norwich was! Norwich is hardly a hidden village in the Outback of Australia, you know!"

"There, there, I'm sure Mr. Marlowe's not a Welshman. He speaks with an educated home-county accent."

"My point exactly. Why put on the airs of a middle-class education if you don't know the geography a schoolboy would need to know to get out of the lower forms? Mark my words, Phoebe, he's a ruddy valet or footman who learned his manners from his betters and probably had to leave England after he committed a terrible crime!"

Bertie brightened as a new thought hit him and he announced, "I say, Marlowe could be Jack the Ripper! They never caught Saucy Jack, you know, and it's only been a few years since he gave up his disgusting habits in the East End! What do you think, captain?"

Captain Gringo laughed as he stared out across the water at the sad dejected figure sitting in the stranded White before he said, "If Marlowe had ever been Jack the Ripper, Jack the Ripper would have been caught."

Everyone laughed but Sylvia. He decided he liked old Phoebe better, even if she wasn't as pretty. It was a waste of God's time to create beautiful women with brooding dispositions. He suspected that even if he could get next to Sylvia he'd regret it in the cold gray dawn. Moody bitches were only fun going *in*. Getting *out* could get tedious as hell.

Major Wallace came their way, holding one end of a manila line he was uncoiling from under the rear of his own steam car. He nodded at them and said, "Got my fire going again. Must say these little flash boilers build pressure quickly."

He moved to the river's edge until his boots were starting to sink in the mud before he called out, "Hoy, Marlowe! Wade in and take this line."

Out on the river, Marlowe called back, "I'll get wet!"

Wallace yelled, "That's the smartest thing you've said all day! Of course you'll get wet, you idiot! Who the flaming hell is supposed to get wet for you, *me?* Not bloody likely! You stalled out there. Come in and take this line!"

As the remittance man stepped warily down into the waist-deep water, the major growled in a lower tone, "I'd leave the sod, if it weren't for the car and its supplies. Must say he's a fair driver. Can't understand how he managed to stall out there, though."

Captain Gringo told the major about Gaston's plan to leave the old trail and try for a run between the jungle trees. Wallace frowned and said, "Doubt it'll work, but it's worth a try. If we can't get the machines between the big stuff, we can always work back to the trail and merrily mow our way through the lighter second growth."

Sylvia protested, "Not while I'm driving the lead car! Half the shattered branches landed in my lap just now!"

Captain Gringo said, "She's got a point, major. Actually, most of the stuff she flattened fell the other way. But there are tree snakes to consider, and, worse yet, we'll be making one hell of a racket as we push blind thought the gumbo limbo like tin elephants."

Wallace didn't answer right away. Marlowe floundered up the bank and the major handed him the end of the line, saying, "Take this back and make sure you tie it to the frame properly. What are you waiting for, a kiss goodbye? You've delayed us a flaming hour, you stupid bastard!"

Marlowe reddened and started back with the line, head downcast. Captain Gringo didn't blame him. It hadn't been an hour and most of the steamers were still waterlogged. Anyone could get stuck in the mud. The guy had just driven into a soft spot that his wet tires couldn't handle, right?

Major Wallace turned to signal his associate standing by his own car. As the other Englishman bent to start the steam winch, Captain Gringo said, "Hold it! If Marlowe's in mud to his hubs, you could wind up with two cars in the river!"

But the manila line had already snapped taut, and anyone could see that the car stuck in the river was the only one moving. Captain Gringo stared thoughtfully at the red tires of Wallace's machine. The brakes of course would be locked. But Wallace hadn't choked his wheels on the mud and fallen leaves over there. Captain Gringo told Wallace, "When you get him out, take his gun away and hold him here till I get back. No time to explain, but fort your people up between the steam cars and the river!"

And then he was running back to where he'd left Gaston, Pat, and the machine gun. He grabbed the Maxim and kept going, letting the ammo belt lash behind him like the tail of an angry boa. Gaston ran after him, and as he caught up under the trees he gasped, "Who are we after, Dick?"

Captain Gringo snapped, "Not sure yet. Keep it down to a roar and watch the undergrowth to our right!"

He leaped over a fallen forest giant, spotted a shaft of sunlight in the distance, and cut sharply to the west. Gaston had spotted sunlight where sunlight didn't usually grow, too. As he kept pace with his longer-legged comrade he said, "Very clever. They knew we'd scout the ford before we let everyone cross, *non?*"

"Shut up. We'll work around by swinging wider and move in from their rear flank. You were here before; what's just up the trail from the river?"

"You told me to shut up. Besides, I don't remember anything."

Captain Gringo judged they'd moved far enough to the northwest and started moving due east, silent as a cat as his boot heels met only the evil-smelling soggy mat of rotting leaves between the big trees. He saw the pale green glow again and homed in on it. Gaston started to say it looked like someone had macheted a clearing and been camped there sometime, but he didn't. He knew Captain Gringo had it figured.

The ragged line of white-clad ambushers, lined up with their guns trained casually on the gumbo limbo they'd left so considerately for the motorcade to follow, looked like natives as Captain Gringo eyed them over the top of yet another mossy fallen log. Gaston crawled into place at his side and moved the ammo belt to make sure it wouldn't snarl, when and if. The if didn't seem too likely. Gaston grimaced and whispered, "*Ladróns*. Regard those ashes over there behind the last man. They've been here some time. Business must be slow."

"They were waiting for us. Nobody else is expected."

"*Merde alors*, why? The triple-titted treasure is supposed to be up ahead, not on us, yet! What are we waiting for, Dick? Have you for some reason grown fond of that corporal's squad of thieves?"

Captain Gringo shook his head as he sighted along the nine-man line with its exposed right flank to them. He murmured, "It is a corporal's squad, and those are military rifles. Bolt-action repeaters. Makes a guy wonder. How do you figure we take at least one alive?"

"I don't. I do not make it my habit to converse with strange men with guns in their hands."

Before Captain Gringo could answer, they heard two distant gunshots. The ambushers had ears too, so they started to move on the sounds of fire. Captain Gringo didn't want them to, so he fired before they could get out of line. The machine gun cleared its throat with a mad woodpecker death rattle. He had to traverse to hose them all down, since a couple moved like old pros and almost made it to cover before the Maxim fire laid them low.

As the machine gun fell silent, leaving them with ringing ears, Gaston spat and observed, "As I was saying, it is *très* difficult to carry on civilized conversations at times like these. You were right about the military training. That last one you got hit the dirt and rolled like a jolly U.S. Marine!"

Captain Gringo saw he had a third of the belt left. He said, "Stay here and cover me while I see if we had any luck."

They hadn't. As he stepped out in the clearing and started rolling people over, none of them had anything to tell him. He went through the pockets of the dead, getting nothing for his pains but pocket change and sticky fingers. He wiped the blood off on the shirt of the last man down the line, then went back to rejoin Gaston by the log, saying, "That's the trouble with soft-nosed slugs. They kill you almost anywhere they hit you in the trunk. The rifles are Krags."

"U.S. issue?"

"Can't tell. Uncle Sam buys Krags from Sweden because they shoot so good. But the Swedes sell 'em to anyone with the money. The eight-man squad and whoever was their leader all had the same arms and ammo. No I.D. You figure it out, Gaston. You've been a soldier of fortune longer than me."

As Captain Gringo picked up the warm Maxim, Gaston shook his head and said, "I confess it is beyond me, too. Honduran soldiers should have had on Honduran uniforms. Perhaps Nicaraguan rebels?"

"Why pick on us, then? The Nicaraguan establishment wants our heads on a plate, and if rebels knew we were coming . . ."

"Nicaraguan military? Wearing peon cottons and sombreros to avoid an international incident working in another country."

Captain Gringo started walking back to where they'd left the others as he tried that, saw it wouldn't work either, and said, "Nicaraguan troops don't read right. We just came from Nicaragua, damm it."

"Ah, but we were only there long enough to share that blonde."

"Don't talk dirty. That ambush was meant for the Brits we signed on with. If Nicaragua wanted 'em dead, they'd have taken them out while they were fucking around in Puerto Cabezas all that time. Besides, those guys were good. You were right about them moving like guys who'd been under fire before. I read 'em as European- or U.S.-trained."

"They looked like natives, Dick."

"So do you, dressed right for the part. Any dark guy with a good tan looks like a peon in white cotton and straw. None of them looked as Swedish as their guns, but none of them looked particularly Indian, either. Let's drop it for now. Keep your eyes open till we find out who fired those other shots. They sounded like they came from somewhere near the cars."

"*Oui*, but in that case, why only two? Nobody can take out twelve people with two shots, and unless one does, at least ten survivors should be making a lot of noise right now, *non?*"

They found out what had happened when they rejoined the others near the riverbank. Exactly ten people stood around two figures on the ground between Major Wallace's steam car and the one he'd winched out of the river.

Wallace was one of the guys on the ground. The other was Marlowe. Captain Gringo put the Maxim in the rear of Sylvia's Stanley and walked over to join them. He didn't ask if they were dead. He'd seen dead men before. Major Wallace lay on his back with a puzzled expression on his face. Marlowe lay face down with a little whore pistol still gripped in his hand. Captain Gringo asked what had happened. The one called Bertie said, "I shot Marlowe. Had to. The rum bugger whipped his gun out and fired point-blank at the major for no reason at all!"

The girl called Phoebe said, "I think he had a reason. The poor major had just said to put his hands up. I fear there was more to our Mr. Marlowe than met the eye!"

Captain Gringo said that was for sure, as he knelt to roll Marlowe over and go through his pockets. Sylvia asked, "Why was Major Wallace holding him up, for heaven's sake?"

Captain Gringo couldn't ask Marlowe. The remittance man's dead face was covered with mud in place of any expression it might still have worn. Captain Gringo got Marlowe's wallet as he explained, "I told him to, when it occurred to me he'd stalled his car out there on purpose. There was only one reason for him to do that. He wanted to be left behind. Gaston and I just met his friends a quarter mile up the road. You boys and girls were *expected.*"

He opened the wallet. The damned I.D. said that Marlowe was Marlowe. He started going through the other pockets as he added, "In fairness to this slob, he tried to stop you the nice way by getting lost a lot. The ambush up a ways was the backup in case you really got this far. Here's a Swiss army knife. Big deal. You can buy that in any good hardware store. He didn't take any chances about being searched, did he?"

Bertie said, "Oh, I say, why should any of us have suspected him of . . . whatever it was?"

Captain Gringo was too polite to say they'd been taken in like a bunch of greenhorns by a guy they'd never seen before. He stood up, pocketing the nice knife, and stepped over to the major's body. As he knelt to go through the other cadaver's pockets, Sylvia said, "For God's sake, we know who he was! He and my late husband belonged to the same club!"

Captain Gringo took the folded map from Wallace's perforated shirt pocket. To his mild surprise, the "treasure map" was a modern merchant-marine navigational chart printed on linen bond. It, too, had been perforated. As he unfolded it, Marlowe's bullet hole multiplied to a dozen, and the bloodstains didn't do much to make the map legible, either. Captain Gringo grimaced and said, "This poor slob sure got his ticket punched. Is this the only copy of the map?"

Bertie said each driver had been issued a copy by the late major and scampered off to his steam car before Captain Gringo could tell him not to bother. The tall American put the ruined map aside, rolled the body to get at its wallet, and satisfied himself that Wallace had I.D. no sneakier than Marlowe's. But Marlowe had to have been a sneak.

He rose to his feet again and said, "Well, gang, I'd say that tears it. Without a leader, the party's over. You all know the way back to Puerto Cabezas. Gaston and I have private reasons for not going back there, but—"

Sylvia snapped, "Don't be ridiculous. We still have the maps, and what just happened doesn't mean the treasure's been shifted."

A surly male voice in the crowd muttered, "Reasons, indeed! Leave you two up here to look for the perishing treasure on your own? Not bloody likely!"

Sweet little Phoebe said, "Oh, I say, these chaps wouldn't play us false. They don't know where the treasure is!"

Captain Gringo ignored both remarks as he explained, "If there ever was anything worth digging up at Laguna Caratasca, it's long dug. Can't you all see what's just happened? Marlowe joined your expedition to steer you wrong. Those fake guerrillas a quarter mile ahead were waiting to make double-certain. In other words, the other side was on to you before you started!"

The redhead, Pat, of all people, said, "Pooh; if some other chaps beat us to the treasure, why would they have gone to so much trouble to stop us? What poor Major Wallace was after must still be there!"

Sylvia said, "She's right. They may know about the treasure, but they haven't found it yet, Dick. By the way, whom do you suppose they are?"

He shrugged and replied, "Professionals, which is more than you folks can say. Look, you've all got money and nice homes to return to. This has gotten beyond an adventurous lark. The other side is playing for keeps and we don't even know who they are!"

Bertie came back with his own copy of the map and handed it to Captain Gringo already unfolded. As the American scanned it, Sylvia said, "We're pressing on, with or without you and Gaston!"

There was a chorus of agreement as Captain Gringo studied the neatly inked-in additions to the printed blowup of Laguna Caratasca. He whistled wearily, started folding the map again, and said, "Okay, you'd probably never make it back alive alone anyway. We haven't time for an election. So I'm the new numero uno and Gaston is my segundo. Gaston?"

*"Oui?"*

"I'm taking Marlowe's White Steamer for a cover-up joy ride as soon as we can unload the supplies and get up a head of steam. I want you to lead everyone and everything northeast into the big timber at least a couple of miles before you fort up and wait for me there."

Gaston nodded and turned to point at two of the Englishmen, saying, "You and you will assist me in unloading Marlowe's horseless carriage. The rest of you to your vehicles and fire up your boilers, *avec* dispatch!"

One of the Englishmen made the mistake of asking why he had to take orders from a perishing little Frog. So Gaston kicked him in the balls.

As the victim writhed on the ground in pain, Captain Gringo said, "Sorry about that. I forgot to tell you Gaston's used to commanding Foreign Legion thugs. I said there wasn't time for an election and this is not a debating society. We have maybe an hour to get the fuck out of here, if we're lucky. We're up against *pros,* damm it! They had a squad of well-trained riflemen backing Marlowe. So what do you bet they have someone even meaner backing the guys we just took out?"


After Gaston and the others had driven away, Captain Gringo loaded the two bodies into the back of the White Steamer and got in the front with the machine gun. He opened the throttle gingerly and the big steam car responded by lurching forward. He saw that its engine was less responsive than a Stanley's. So much the better. He wanted weight and power, not speed.

He drove over the stubble cleared by Sylvia's push into the gumbo limbo, and when he came to standing saplings, he kept going. He admitted she'd had a point about wanting to drive all the way to the lagoon country through this shit. Most of the trees went down ahead of him as the bumper cut them off near the ground. Some of the springy trunks whipped the wrong way and tried to ride with him. But fortunately they were only a little thicker than broom sticks so he didn't get seriously clubbed.

He leaned into the whipping with his head as low as the steering wheel, following the ruts by feel until he burst out into the clearing where the would-be ambushers had waited. They were still there, with company. A mess of turkey buzzards had settled to feed on the corpses. He braked to a stop and looked away as one helped itself to a juicy eyeball, ignoring him and the steam car.

He turned and said, "This is where you get out," to Marlowe's corpse. He rolled the dead sneak over the side to sprawl artistically in the gumbo limbo stubble. He thought about moving over to the flank to police the brass he'd spilled mowing down the other bodies in the clearing. He grimaced and muttered, "Hell with it. Anyone who can read sign will know these slobs were taken on the flank. If we leave 'em a really interesting trail, they won't bother looking for the few footprints Gaston and I might have left in the dead leaves over there."

He put the steam car in reverse and drove backward in a circle, the way a panic-stricken or wounded driver might have at greater speed. He cut a swath of underbrush, reversed, and made a K turn out into the clearing deliberately to run over a corpse with a squishy bump while he left some tire tracks to read. Then he drove back the way he'd come and ran over Marlowe as long as he was about it. Why make it easy for his friends to recognize the bastard, right?

He drove back near the river and circled around aimlessly to wipe out or confuse the pattern of tracks left earlier by other vehicles. Then he stopped, dragged the dead Wallace up front, and got out. He sat the corpse more or less behind the wheel, picked up his machine gun, and opened the throttle a bit with his free hand. The White Steamer slowly backed into the river. Its firebox hissed and went out as the sluggish water rose to swallow it. But the steam on tap kept the White moving. So Captain Gringo braced the Maxim on his hip and proceeded to shoot the shit out of it. As the boiler blew with a billowing cloud of steam, the big car stopped a dozen yards off shore. He'd used up the rest of the belt. He ejected it and tossed it into the river for the current, such as it was, to carry away.

He surveyed his handiwork. Wallace slumped nicely over the wheel out there as Captain Gringo put himself in another's boots and murmured, "Let's see, they drove into the ambush as planned, but the wise-ass sons of bitches had flank scouts out on foot and it was a mutual disaster. The agent we planted in the expedition bought the farm. The leader was hit in the shootout and only made it to here, but it sure looks like the others made it back across the Segovia. By now they'd have made it back to Puerto Cabezas, and then . . .? Shit, why worry about them?"

He hefted the spent machine gun to his shoulder and picked up a snapped-off sapling before following the tire tracks Gaston and the others had left cutting into the woods. As he walked backward out of the clearing near the river, he swept soggy dead leaves into meaningless patterns with his heavy improvised broom. It was hard work in this humid heat, but he made sure there were no tire tracks within a city block of the clearing before he dropped the sapling, turned, and followed the remaining tracks.

It wasn't as easy as it might have been. At Gaston's direction, Sylvia's lead car had zigzagged for the high and dry between the buttress roots of the big timber, and the soggy forest duff had sprung or oozed to heal its furrowed surface. He'd have lost the trail if he hadn't known it was there and the general direction they'd taken. But after he'd walked a million weary miles with the heavy Maxim and was cursing Gaston for driving off so fucking far, he spotted the side of a steam car ahead between the trees. Better yet, Gaston had posted a perimeter and he was challenged by Bertie as he came in. As they met, Bertie said, "Oh, sorry. We've assigned Phoebe to drive Wallace's steamer. Wilson didn't do so well getting here. Don't know if he's less experienced or if it was the kick in the nuts."

Captain Gringo made a mental note that the possible troublemaker was named Wilson. He'd memorize the other names when he had time for contemplation. He moved on, saw that Gaston had drawn the big vehicles into a wagon laager, and heaved the Maxim into the back of Sylvia's Stanley with a sigh of relief as the others joined him, babbling all at once.

He nodded approvingly at the extra gear now strapped neatly to the Stanley, but said, "Don't bunch up, damm it."

Gaston elbowed through to say, *"Merde alors*, Dick, are you expecting an artillery shelling?"

Captain Gringo said, "Don't know. They had mighty up-to-date rifles. Okay, as long as the gang's all here, I think I left them a false trail. The reason for all these dramatics was on your maps. Professional draftsmen inked those printed charts for Wallace. I'd say that was where he made his first mistake. A journeyman draftsman doesn't make enough to live on in London if he likes booze and broads enough to matter. The poor dumb Wallace had them ink in the words *Treasure Trove* on at least five charts, and anyone can read *Laguna Caratasca* when it's printed halfway across a damned navigational chart! One of the draftsmen made a private copy to show his drinking buddies. Jack the Ripper can't be the only criminal London's ever seen. So you kiddies weren't the only gang recruited to go treasure hunting. Damn, I wish Wallace hadn't bought the farm! He left us with so many loose ends!"

He turned to Sylvia and said, "Tell me more about Wallace, Sylvia."

She said, "I thought I had. He rowed for Harrow and belonged to my late husband's club. I assure you he was socially acceptable."

"Where did he get that major's rank?"

She looked blank. Bertie said, "Indian Army, retired, he said."

"Retired, Bertie? The guy couldn't have been much more than thirty-five or so."

"Well, now that I think about it, I do believe there was some sort of a row. Chap at the club said Wallace had gotten into some sort of sticky wicket in the Punjab and been allowed to retire for the good of the service or some such rot. Sorry, don't have any details to offer. By the way, I do hope he was buried properly back there?"

"I disposed of both the bodies properly," said Captain Gringo, which was true, when you studied it. He said, "All right, we'll sort out the small print later. Right now we'd better put some more distance between our butts and whomsoever. Gaston, how tough was it driving through this tall timber?"

Gaston said, "Formidable, but not as impossible as I expected at first. I frankly thought you were mad to suggest driving through a jungle in horseless carriages. I always thought they had been designed with paved roads in mind."

"Let's hope that's what the other side thinks. Sylvia, do you have a pocket compass?"

"No, but there's a compass on the dashboard. Didn't you notice?"

"No. Who looks at dials when cops are shooting at you? With dashboard compasses, this gets even better. You sure can't navigate by the sun, down here under all this spinach. Okay, everyone mount up and follow us. We're going for a drive in the country."

Nobody argued. Nobody wanted to be kicked in the balls. As he got in with Gaston, Pat, and Sylvia, he said, "Drive due west, doll."

Sylvia started the Stanley and swung the wheel as he'd told her to, but objected, "Why are we headed for the Pacific, Dick?"

He explained, "We can't get there from here. Honduras is too bumpy away from the coastal lowlands. Anyone trailing us will be afoot, or at best aboard a bronc, and horses need lots of rest in the tropics. The plan is to drive so far that nobody can possibly catch up before we've taken time to rest up, sort things out, and plan our next move. You were right about the seaward approaches to the lagoon being guarded. Wallace was an old military hand and had the standard marks for gun emplacements inked in. Unless he had a vivid imagination, somebody on the other side sure has lots of money and a private army. Where Wallace screwed up was in marking his own sneaky landward approach. The trail we just left wasn't on the original charts until he had it inked in. Assuming the other side has a copy, we don't want to approach the lagoon anywhere near that damn trail! If our luck holds out we may be able to swing around through the jungle in a wide circle and come in from the northwest, which would surprise the hell out of me if I were holding the lagoon right now. The lagoon runs nearly fifty miles along the Mosquito Coast. A force big enough to have every approach covered would be big enough to take all of Honduras, so why fool around with hidden treasure?"

At his side in the back, Gaston said, *"Eh bien,* but Laguna Caratasca is not our target, Dick. We know where that was without Wallace's map. Did the map pinpoint the treasure?"

"Of couse not. The other side wouldn't still be looking for whatever Wallace was after if he'd been *that* dumb. There's a two-mile-square area just north of the end of the old trail where he was dumb enough to letter in 'Area of the Buried Treasure.' Where was that old pirate camp?"

"In the area he outlined, of course. I am beginning to see the light. Wallace didn't know the exact location himself. He just knew where the coastal pirates used to hide out between sea forays. He heard or, worse yet, assumed some of them buried some loot before they were shelled to premature retirement by Queen Victoria's adorable gunboats. It is my understanding that they did not content themselves with pounding the pirates from the sea. After they pulverized the camp, they sent landing parties in to mop up. The pirates may not have been in condition to discuss buried treasure with the Royal Marines, but it seems to me the heavy shelling should have unearthed anything that was not buried *très* deep, *non?"*

Captain Gringo smiled thinly and said, "That works even better. Wallace was a military man and marines talk to soldiers if they're buying the drinks. Try it this way. The pirates didn't bury anything. Like you said, why should they have?"

Gaston nodded and said, *"Oui, les* Royal Marines are paid better than my gay old Legion, but not *that* much more. Let us say one or more of the landing party found some goodies in the ruins, shoved them into a shell crater, and kicked as much sand in atop the loot as they could manage before their officers got wise! It falls together much better than a barefoot Captain Kidd, *non?"*

"All except the amount involved. We can't be talking about even a chest of coins, Gaston. Look at the money represented in this rolling stock alone! And the other side has field guns dug in to guard the seaward approaches while they do their own looking, for God's sake! Sylvia, did Wallace tell you or the others how much money was involved?"

She steered wide of a big quinine tree before answering, "Not in exact figures. But he said we'd each get at least ten quid back for each one we put in. My own investment was two thousand pounds, if that's your next question."

It had been. Captain Gringo whistled thoughtfully. Sylvia's investment alone came to ten thousand dollars in real money. And Wallace had sold the idea to, let's see, ten people, not counting himself and the late Marlowe. Assuming they'd all invested about the same amount, Wallace had raised at least a hundred grand before they'd left England!

Gaston had been counting too. He said, *"Eh bien,* it could not have been the game of con. With a fortune like that in his hot little hands, Wallace could simply have run off to Tahiti and lived happily ever after, *non?"*

"Okay, so what's worth a million that you can shove in a hole in a hurry? He promised a ten-to-one return, and that's what she adds up to in round figures!"

Gaston shrugged and said, "Not gold. A million in gold specie would be *très* heavy, and we are assuming a hasty burial. Besides, had the unwashed coastal pirates gathered a million—and I don't see how—why would they have been there waiting to be wiped out by the Royal Navy? As I said, they were bush-league riffraff, not followers of the great Morgan."

The redhead, Pat, turned in her seat by Sylvia to offer, "Diamonds? Those uncouth ruffians may have relieved some poor señorita of jewels they didn't know the value of. Perhaps a family treasure, ripped from the heaving breast of a poor frightened girl in inexpensive clothes, since she was living in genteel poverty and . . ."

"Hey, don't make up a romance novel, Pat!" Captain Gringo cut in with a laugh, adding, "You could be on to something, leaving out the dramatic trimmings we'll probably never know in detail. It works more than one way, damm it. The pirates may well have had something they didn't know the value of. On the other hand, a couple of marines may have made an awful mistake with the rhinestones of some pirate's *adelita!* I can't see even Queen Victoria sending assault troops ashore with jeweler's loupes screwed to their eyes, and it takes a pro to tell real jewelry from good paste!"

Gaston said, "I vote we drive on to Patuca, the next port up the coast. I think we can make it by horseless carriage, and, more important, it is a small but adorable out-of-the-way port where we could no doubt catch a passing schooner long before the *alcalde* could get word to the capital that a bunch of maniacs had just driven into his town from the jungle."

Gaston always said things like that, so Captain Gringo didn't answer. But Sylvia's jaw was stubbornly set as she said, "See here, I have too much invested to give up now!"

Pat said, "Me too. I know all too well about genteel poverty. I had to borrow my share from a beastly maiden aunt who's never going to let me live it down should I return empty-handed. I'll be keeping house for the old bawd the rest of my perishing life!"

They rounded a giant mahogany to see an even bigger tree stretched out across their route. Sylvia braked to a stop and said, "Blast. Which way around is shorter?"

Captain Gringo said, "Hold it. The ground slopes down beyond that windfall, and when the ground dips here, it gets even muddier. How far have we driven, Sylvia?"

She looked at her instrument panel and said, "Almost fifteen miles. Why?"

"Swing due north. We'll follow this rise another ten and make camp."

She started the way indicated, but protested, "We've plenty of daylight left, Dick."

He said, "I know. I want to know where the hell we are when we stop. Twenty-five miles into the trees should be about right, and I mean to make a comfortable dry camp, so we may have to scout around for a good rise with water within reach. We'll be staying there awhile."

Pat asked, "We're camping in this uncharted wilderness more than a few hours, Dick?"

He said, "You bet your sweet fanny we are. I want to give the other side time to assume we've left for good before we move any closer in on 'em!"

Gaston nudged him and shot him a silent frown as the two girls stared ahead. Captain Gringo grinned but nodded encouragement. He knew Gaston had seen the redhead first, the bastard.

Sylvia was even prettier. But they didn't seem to be hitting it off. He supposed that, having married up to Belgravia, she was no longer interested in guys who didn't wear neckties and hadn't rowed for Harrow. Nobody was as big a snob as a snob who'd started out poor, and he didn't like snobs of any background. So, damm it, Gaston figured to get laid in the near future and Captain Gringo was already feeling left out!

They made camp on what was probably a lonely island in the rainy season. The ground sloped gently away between the close-ranked trees on all sides. A quarter mile away, a sluggish little stream of tea-colored water wound mysteriously from nowhere to anywhere through the jungle. Some of the others wanted to camp closer to water. Some of the others hadn't camped in mosquito country before.

Captain Gringo would have ordered them to pitch their tents at least two miles from the nearest water if that had been possible in this soggy stretch of rain forest. Mosquitoes ranged a little over a mile from where they'd hatched. He hoped that not many had, in the nearby stream. The water was moving and minnows darted about under the surface. The water was stained by tannin from the trees all around, not from silt, and the two soldiers of fortune had learned that neither mosquitoes nor the more dangerous organisms of tropic dysentery liked to dwell in acid water.

Like everything else about the crazy English expedition, the tents and camping gear Wallace had bought with other people's money added up to no spared expenses. Captain Gringo remembered how upset the Duke of Wellington had been when his junior officers unfurled those umbrellas at the Battle of Waterloo. For an exploring race, limeys sure took along lots of the comforts of home.

But hell, he enjoyed comfort too, and since old Wallace had no further use for it, he commandeered the dead leader's tent. It was a gasser. Thick rubberized canvas formed a nice dry floor, and there was room enough inside to hold a tea party, if he'd had any friends. Gaston had encountered no resistance as he'd helped Pat set up her tent. But Captain Gringo detected a certain reserve from the others, now that he'd taken command. It hardly seemed fair. Gaston was the one who'd kicked Wilson in the nuts. But it was always lonely at the top. Maybe it was just British reserve.

Aside from Bertie and the now recovered Wilson, a rather dour Scot even when he wasn't nursing a bruised ball, the other male survivers, now that he'd had time to learn their names, were called Baxter, Gordon, Fenton and Jerome.

He hadn't figured out if Jerome was the guy's first or last name. It hardly mattered. Jerome was a little shriveled-up guy with not much to distinguish him but an enlarged Adam's apple, which he kept swallowing as he refused to meet anyone's eyes. It seemed he had some sort of nervous tic that made him gulp like that. It was Jerome's problem, thank God.

Nobody argued as Captain Gringo directed them to build a fire in the middle of the encircled tents. He explained that after they'd used the fire to cook the last meal of the day, he meant to pile lots of forest duff on the coals to leave it smoking but not showing after dark. The smoke would help with the bugs. It was nobody else's business where said fire might be. All the tents had netting, of course, so there was a fifty-fifty chance they wouldn't be completely drained of blood by morning.

The women took over the cooking chores without being told to, bless them. By now he knew them well enough to call them Sylvia, Pat, Phoebe, and Matilda. Matilda was the big tough dame who said "shit" in an upper-class accent the queen might have envied.

By desperately casual questioning during the day he'd established that all four dames were more or less unattached. Matilda had a husband back in Kensington, apparently left behind to water her plants and keep an eye on the servants while she was off treasure hunting on her own. He could see why her old man hadn't objected too hard. She wasn't exactly unattractive, but, in addition to cussing like a man, she moved like a tall youth in skirts and would have bossed hell out of the other girls if they'd paid any attention to her.

As they put the high tea on the fire, Captain Gringo took Bertie aside, since he seemed to think on his feet pretty well despite the Oxford that came out of his ruddy face. The American said, "You know more than me about Wallace. But before we talk about him, what can you tell me about the fuel situation? I've only seen the spare kerosene tins in the back of Sylvia's steamer. Had I been Wallace, I'd have brought a lot more."

"I say, how was he to know we'd be driving all over the map? I'm sure we've enough to get to the lagoon, even after this wide detour."

"Okay, then what? Didn't Wallace plan on driving back? I don't think Sylvia has enough spare fuel. Unless the rest of you have twice as much as she started out with, you don't have enough either."

"Oh, well, as I said, we never expected all this extra mileage."

"Will you listen with both ears, Bertie? We wouldn't have gotten to Laguna Caratasca yet if we'd driven straight down that original path. Sylvia's fuel is already more than half used up. I know it's not cricket to speak ill of the dead, but Wallace couldn't have been planning to come back by horseless carriage, see?"

"Oh, I say, I certainly do now! I confess I feel rather silly, too. Of course we let Major Wallace do all the logistical planning. Until you mentioned it just now, I hadn't even considered whether I had enough kerosene or not. Whatever do you imagine he had in mind?"

"A double-cross, maybe. One car could make it easy on the tins left in the other four. Three, now. Gaston was smart enough to toss the extra fuel from the White into other vehicles, but there's still not enough."

"I say, that couldn't have been Wallace's plan. The rest of us would have raised a bit of a row, you know."

"Yeah, if any of you were alive."

"Good God, what a beastly idea! Are you suggesting Wallace intended to do us all in after using us to find what he was looking for?"

"It's happened. But if Wallace had been that slick with a gun, Marlowe never would have beaten him to the draw. You managed to nail Marlowe, and I notice the other men and that big butch Matilda are wearing sidearms. So let's talk about the others. Wallace couldn't have planned to knock off so many people without help. Marlowe obviously wasn't in cahoots with him. He recruited Gaston and me knowing we were professional fighting men. I'd say it'd take at least three guns, crossfire, to do the job right, even if the rest of us were caught flat-footed. What's the story on Wilson, for openers?"

"Oh, it couldn't be Wilson, he's related to the Duke of Caithness and played rugby as a lad. He's a bit of a brawler and has a beastly temper when he's been drinking. He's a Scot, you see, but nonetheless a proper gentleman. I've played cards with him many a time."

"How's he fixed for money?"

"Oh, he's oozing with it. I said he was a Scot, and even if he *did* spend lavishly, he owns a distillery in Glen Spey. He'd never murder anyone for money."

"Maybe he could have another reason. Who's Baxter?"

"Oh, Freddy? He went up to Oxford with me. Didn't graduate, of course. Something about riding his horse through the dean's marigolds one night. He's a bit queer in other ways. Has a bachelor flat in Mayfair and seems to like rosy-cheeked boys, but he's never murdered any of them as far as anyone knows. He oozes money, too. Family owns a shipyard or something."

"Was Wallace a queer?"

"Good Lord, do you suppose I ever *asked?* Wait, he couldn't have been. As I recall his trouble in the Indian army, it involved another officer's wife."

"Okay, some guys swing both ways, but we'll put Baxter on the back of the stove for now. Who's Gordon?"

"Another Scot, of course. Highlander. Not as dour as Wilson. Given to singing songs about Bonny Prince Charlie when he's had a bit too much at the club. His people are no longer Catholic, of course. George the Third converted all the Jacobite clans by giving them back their kilts in exchange for switching to the High Kirk. Let's see, I think Gordon's related to the Earl of Huntley. He likes girls, as all Highlanders seem to. Never met a queer Highlander, now that I think about it. I rather imagine being raised in kilts has something to do with it, although I can't see why. At any rate, you can forget Jock Gordon as a Murderer. Turned down a commission in the family regiment to devote his time to raising milch kine on his family estates. That's estates in the plural, by the way. He sells milk to half the country. In tins of course. Gordon Condensed Milk."

"I've seen the label on many a can. Okay, I know this is silly, but what about Jerome?"

"Good God, he's a religious fanatic. Welsh chapel. Family is in coal. Not really *in* the coal, of course. They sell it, in Cardiff. He's a rather silly twit but filthy rich. I say, we seem to have run out of chaps and none of them fits your grim picture, what?"

"Neither did Wallace, but the more I study him the more I smell a rat. I know about Sylvia and Pat. Who's your little chum with the glasses?"

"Phoebe Chambers? Lord, I wish she were my little chum. Tried, of course. I don't seem to be her type. The sad part is, she's supposed to be a bit of a bawd, despite her sedate looks. Saw her in a bathing dress at Brighton once and, well, those glasses don't tell the whole story. As a suspect for *other* transgressions, Phoebe won't do. She has a very good income left her by a father who mucked about in Australian wool. Not in the wool itself of course, but . . ."

"Right, he sold lots of wool and left her lots of money. You say she has a rep for round heels? Could she have been laying down a lot for old Wallace?"

"How on earth should I know a thing like that? She's never invited me to her bedroom, with or without other company present. I don't think they were lovers, though. Must say I was rather surprised, after the stories I'd heard about her. She runs with a rather fast crowd from Bloomsbury, although she lives in a better neighborhood, of course."

Captain Gringo said, "Maybe she's picky, or maybe someone just talks nasty about a lady with bohemian leanings. Who's Matilda and how come her husband couldn't make it?"

"Oh, she's quite mad. *He* must be too. They have one of those marriages of convenience. Both from titled families, so they never got to choose. He's a Cecil. She's a Harcourt. The old boy has a seat in Lords and makes all sorts of things out of steel in the Black Country. The people who work for him do, that is. They live between the Palace and Marble Arch, on Park Row, when they're in London. Never been to their country place in Cornwall. Hear it's seven thousand acres under cultivation with a great swamping moor for birding. She's a jolly good shot. But as far as I know she's never shot anything but birds. On the wing of course. Can't see her shooting *me*. We get along quite well, as a matter of fact."

"Yeah, and Sylvia says *you* have more money than brains."

"Did she? I say, I'm not sure if that's a compliment or not. In all modesty, I do have a rather decent income. Bonds backed by the Old Lady of Threadneedle Street and a few shares in Lloyd's. The bank, not the insurance chaps. Don't ask me how the devil stocks and bonds work. I just have to clip the coupons and send them in whenever I have bills to pay. It seems to pile up faster than I can spend it. Never have understood why."

Captain Gringo left Bertie to ponder his unfortunate fate. The still confused American moved over to Sylvia's steamer, parked with the others outside the tent circle, and was cleaning the bore of the Maxim when Gaston joined him.

The Frenchman sat on the running board to mutter darkly, "*Sacre* God damn, Pat is sharing her tent with that Sylvia. Why do I do such mad things, Dick? After investing all that charm on the redhead, I learn the big buck-toothed Matilda insisted on her own private tent! Do you think it is too late to start a new campaign?"

Captain Gringo said it was worth a try. Maybe Gaston was too big a chump to see that if Matilda slept alone, it left Phoebe in another private tent as well. On the other hand, Phoebe couldn't be as easy a lay as she was reputed to be, if she was still sleeping alone, and he had more important things to worry about. A guy could always get laid, sooner or later, but if somebody killed you, you didn't even get to jerk off for one hell of a long time.

He filled Gaston in on his suspicions. Gaston agreed with them and asked in a more serious than usual tone what the hell they were doing with this bunch of misfits. He added, "Whatever Wallace planned and whatever he was after is ancient history, Dick. Even if there is a treasure worth the time of people who already have money to burn, and even if that *très* suspicious Wallace had left an X to mark the spot, there seems to be a gang sitting on it. A big one, with *cannon*, for God's sake!"

"Hey, I said the whole story was nuts, Gaston. Meanwhile, it got us out of Nicaragua one jump ahead of the firing squad, so what the hell. I'm open to suggestions, but did you have someplace better to go?"

"*Oui;* I told you there was a *très* discreet seaport just up the coast on the far side of the big lagoon."

"I know. I found Patuca on the map. Even if I could talk the others into it, Patuca's too far. We don't have enough kerosene. We've barely enough to make Laguna Caratasca."

"*Merde alors*, have the humming birds built nests in your ears? That's where the other gang is. The ones with all the big guns!"

"Yeah, and unless they like to read in the dark, a lot of fuel oil. These boilers will run on any kind of liquid fuel from kerosene to coconut oil. Those other guys must have supplies. Both these crazy expeditions are well funded. Too well funded for any sensible reason I can come up with, but we'll find the answers over by the old pirate camp, not in Patuca."

"You are suffering sunstroke, despite the forest gloom, Dick. That rifle squad we took out was not made up of fruity rich Englishmen and four women for God's sake! The only person on our side who looks at all tough is that big Matilda. These people are rank amateurs! Even if they were not, there are only a dozen of us to God knows what, *hein?*"

"That's one of the things we'll find out when we get there. Don't you have any curiosity, Gaston? Hell, for all we know, we scared them worse than they scared us! Those nine we took out might have been most of their strength."

"*Sacre bleu,* don't shit my bull, Dick. Wallace marked out *gun positions* on both sides of the lagoon entrance. Cannon come with cannoneers. The one's we brushed with were infantry. *Trained* infantry, despite their casual dress. Nobody hires a mere squad of infantry. The basic unit is a company."

"For God's sake, you've been talking to Pat too much. You're starting to sound dramatic, too. Wallace didn't recruit any goddamn company, or even a serious platoon. They're probably common criminals. Okay, so some may have deserted an army some time ago. There can't be any official military units in the area. Honduras and Nicaragua are not at war this season, and if anyone *else* was invading, both countries would be yelling to Uncle Sam about the Monroe Doctrine by now. I read the papers back in Puerto Cabezas while we were screwing around to kill time that afternoon. There was not a word about any international crisis calling for anybody's military intervention, and remember, Wallace planned this caper months in advance. The other side must have too, to beat him here."

"*Merde alors,* who cares? If we helped ourselves to one of the steam cars and loaded it up with extra fuel tins . . ."

"Hold it!" Captain Gringo cut in, adding, "That's pretty shitty, even from you, Gaston. I thought you liked Pat."

"Not enough to *die* for her! There are times a man must be *practique.*"

"Your idea isn't practical. It's murder. How long would these poor greenhorns last in this jungle if we deserted them?"

"Long enough to walk back to Puerto Cabezas, if they had any sense."

"They don't. I've already suggested they turn back. They won't. Nothing is as stubborn as ten grand invested for a hundred. Break open an ammo canister and hand me a belt, will you? I'll leave this one here and put the other on the far side if it doesn't come out of its case too rusty. Guess who gets to take turns with me on perimeter guard tonight."

"*Merde*, I'd never be able to sleep with any of these other halfwits standing guard. Regard that species of Matilda waving imperiously over by the fire. Let us see if the food is better than Wallace's other weird plans. It can't be any worse, *non?*"

Captain Gringo was awakened by a hair-raising scream. So he sat up in his sleeping bag with pillow gun in hand before he figured out what it was. Then he sighed and lay back down, naked, to tuck the .38 away. A jaguar had been singing to its lady love in the jungle. The big spotted cats did that a lot, but they seldom came close to the smell of gun oil, and what the hell, Gaston was out there prowling, too.

The big Yank didn't check the time. Gaston had his own watch and he knew all too well that the Frenchman would wake him with worse noises than a jungle cat when it was his turn at bat.

The canvas above him rippled gently as a mysterious night breeze swept between the big trees all around. That probably meant rain before morning. Meanwhile it had gotten comfortably cool. Had he left a tarp over the one good gun outside? Yeah, he had. The other son-of-a-bitching Maxim had been wasted freight. If Wallace had been alive when he'd opened the crate after supper, he'd probably have been as chagrined.

You were supposed to ship weapons in oil, not rust. He'd cleaned and pocketed a few spare parts just in case. Most of the action had been shot after some stupid bastard packed the gun without cleaning and greasing it after it had last been fired.

He heard his tent flap open. He couldn't see who had entered but assumed it was Gaston. So he was surprised when whoever it was got under the sheets with him, naked. He knew it couldn't be Gaston, even if Gaston had gone nuts. Gaston didn't have such nice tits.

He took whoever she was in his arms, since he couldn't think of any better way to greet her. She snuggled closer to whisper, "I'm so frightened! What was that dreadful noise just now?"

He said, "Jaguar. Big pussy cat. And speaking of pussies . . ."

"Sir! What on earth are you doing to my privates?" she demanded. Which was a pretty silly question coming from a naked lady in a bed roll with a naked gentleman. So he didn't answer. He just rolled atop her, wedged her naked thighs open with his knees, and got into her with no further bullshit. She gasped, stiffened, then wrapped her legs around his waist as she protested, "This wasn't why I came in here, damm it! Do you always rape helpless women who thought they could trust you?"

"Every chance I get," he replied, thrusting deeper into her warm wet interior. She was tight as hell, and must have noticed. She moaned, "Oh, you're too big. I can't stand it. This is so humiliating and, ah, could you move a little faster, you brute?"

He did, and she said, "That's better. As long as a poor girl has to get raped she may as well enjoy it."

Whoever the hell she was, she seemed to enjoy it very much indeed, and now that they were such good friends she commenced to run her nails up and down his spine while she tongued him deeply and drummed on his naked butt with her naked heels. He enjoyed it, too. It had been some time since he'd had anything half as good, and the fact that he had no idea which of the four girls in camp she might be added to the adventure. He took turns picturing her as Sylvia, Pat, Phoebe, and Matilda. No, not old Matilda. Matilda was too big and rangy. But what the hell, even a three-woman fantasy harem was a lot of fun.

He was mentally laying the redhead when she stretched her legs out to both sides and gasped, "Deeper, deeper, I'm *coming!*"

So he changed her to the brooding dark Sylvia and came in her at the same time. They went weakly limp in each other's arms and she said, "Oh, you're just dreadful. I never intended a thing like this to happen, Dick."

"Is that why you came in here naked and attacked me?"

"Don't be beastly, dearest. I was half-asleep and scared out of my wits by that terrible tiger scream." She giggled coyly and added, "I suppose I'll have to forgive you. Now that I'm awake I can see how you must have mistaken my visit for an improper advance. Uh, now that the damage has been done, do you suppose we could do it some more?"

He rolled partly off her and groped for his shirt in the dark as he replied, "In a minute. I didn't hold back at all so I need to catch my second wind. Let's just share a smoke and some cuddles and . . ."

"Don't strike a light!" she pleaded. But the damage had been done. As he lit his cigar she looked away, shame-faced. He shook out the light, held the cigar aside to kiss her reassuringly, and said, "Why, Miss Phoebe, I hardly recognized you without your glasses."

"Oh, how will I ever face you and the others in the light of day?"

"Well, I don't know about me, but I won't tell if you won't tell."

"You promise, Dick? I'd just die if the other girls knew I was so evil!"

"Hey, you're not evil. You're just warm-natured. Come to think of it, I smoke too much."

He snuffed out the smoke and held her closer as she protested, "I feel so low, Dick!"

"That's because you're on the bottom. Want to get on top?"

"That's not what I meant. I meant . . . Oh, God, I don't know what I meant, that perishing great cock feels so good in me. But you must promise never to tell a soul!"

He shut her up by kissing her again. She sure talked silly for a gal who screwed so sensibly. He knew, now, that Bertie had been right about the rumors he'd heard about her and her bohemian friends. She probably made some of them promise not to talk when she went slumming. But naturally Blooms-bury blokes didn't get a crack at many high-born ladies, so someone had bragged, the dumb prick. He knew that if he had something like this all to himself, he'd keep it all to himself.

They shared another orgasm, and now that she'd dropped the act she took him up on his suggestion that she get on top. He'd meant for her to screw him in that position. The secret little bawd had naughtier views on love. But what the hell, they'd both had a chance to clean off since they'd last been with anyone else, and eating a lady who was eating you seemed only common courtesy. So they were going sixty-nine hot and heavy when the flap opened—in the dark, thank God—and Gaston said, "Dick?"

Phoebe turned to stone atop him, his organ grinder still between her pursed lips as he growled, "Gaston, don't you ever knock? Go find your own girl, dammit!"

Gaston said, "I didn't find a girl. I found a boy. An Indian. You'd better come out here and talk to him. His friends are all around us in the dark!"


It hardly seemed fair to call the Mosquito Indians Mos-quitoes, or Moskitoes as some purists spelled it. For one thing, while they were little guys, they weren't *that* little. And they didn't sting as often, though some said they stung anyone who bothered them, with the long reed arrows they shot from bows taller than they were.

The Indian standing outside with Gaston had politely left his weapons in the jungle before coming in for a pow wow. Since Mosquitoes didn't have much else but their weapons, he was stark naked, unless the red paint on his dangling penis counted as formal attire in these parts.

Captain Gringo of course had hurriedly dressed before coming out to see what was up. He hoped Phoebe had sense enough to get up and out of his tent on her own before any of the others noticed. The other members of the expedition were coming in from all sides to join them and it seemed to be making the young Indian edgy, so Captain Gringo called out, "Okay, everyone back to their tents. This is a private conversation. I hope."

The Indian didn't understand the English words, but smiled at the results. Captain Gringo smiled at him, held out a cigar, and asked, *"Habla usted Español?"*

Gaston murmured, "He doesn't speak Spanish, I tried some on him."

The young Indian gravely accepted the tobacco and sniffed it before he spoke in a lingo that consisted mostly of mournful groans and high-pitched birdcall imitations.

Captain Gringo got a word here and there, or thought he might have. He'd shacked up with more than one Maya and been very good friends with a San Blas sorceress one time, and, after all, how many kinds of noises could any Indian make?

When he'd finished his oration, the young Indian put the cigar in his mouth. So Captain Gringo lit it for him. He didn't seem surprised at the match flare. So he'd dealt with whites before. He blew smoke in Captain Gringo's face, did the same favor for Gaston, and turned to walk away without another word. Gaston started to object, but Captain Gringo said,

"Don't grab him. We're being watched. Why is that fucking fire going? I told you I didn't want to advertise our where-abouts, dammit!"

Gaston said, "I didn't do that. *He* did. I was walking the perimeter and never suspected his presence until the species of savage was kicking the leaves off the coals as if he lived here! *Merde alors,* such manners!"

Captain Gringo nodded and said, "He has *good* manners, when you consider how he might have gotten us to notice him! I don't know what the hell the message was, just now. But I don't think they're mad at us."

"*Sacrebleu.* He sounded like he was giving birth to a broken bottle. What happens now, Dick?"

"Good question. It seems to be up to them. I'll stay here in sight. You stroll casually to each tent and tell everyone to keep their guns handy but to stay out of sight. I remember a similar occasion in Apache country one night. It turned out they wanted to have a man-to-man fight between me and a war chief, but this could turn out a nicer way."

Gaston shrugged and stepped away from the faint glow of the fire. Captain Gringo kicked a couple of pieces of fresh kindling on to make it burn brighter as he sat down by it, took out another cigar, and lit up.

It felt like only a couple of hours as he sat there wondering what a reed arrow in the back felt like. They said the poison on the tip killed quickly and painlessly. Actually it was only about ten minutes before the same Indian kid came back with an old wrinkled guy and a young girl about eleven years old, judging by her bare pubis. Her breasts were those of a full-grown woman, though. The three naked Indians squatted across the fire from him as he pretended to ignore them. It wasn't easy, looking at a naked lady's slit as she squatted with her knees apart like that. The old man had a parrot feather in his iron-gray hair and his pecker was painted green. That probably made him important. He was smoking the kid's cigar, too. It was odd how almost all Indians shared the same tobacco culture. He supposed that as tobacco had been passed from tribe to tribe in the old days, the rituals that went with it had been passed along as well. So far he'd never been scalped by an Indian who'd accepted a smoke from him, but there was always a first time.

The old man said something to the girl that sounded dreadfully insulting. She nodded and said in Spanish, "The *brujo* wishes to know if you and your friends are wicked people. He says to tell you we are not savage people. But if you are wicked, he warns you he has many curses to sing over your images."

Captain Gringo blew a thoughtful smoke cloud and said, "That sounds fair and reasonable. Tell your *brujo* I respect and fear his powers, but that I don't think he should curse me before he knows me better."

The girl repeated his words in Mosquito and the old man favored him with a sinister smile. Medicine men did that a lot. Most of them were afraid that whites would tell them they were full of shit, and it never hurt to flatter one's elders.

The old man gargled razor blades at the girl awhile before she smiled across the fire at the tall blond American and explained, "The *brujo* says the spirits told him you had not come to harm us, since how could you have known we were here? Now he wishes to know if you are friends of the strangers over by the big salt water."

He was only half-faking when he pretended to choose his words carefully, as Indians preferred. His visitors hadn't said what *their* current relationship to the other side was. Unfortunately, most Indians were smart enough to tell when you were beating around the bush, and didn't like it. He took the bull by the horns and said, "Hear me; I know little about those other *blancos* camped near Laguna Caratasca. My friends and I were going there when they started shooting at us for some reason. As you see, we have run deep into the forest to decide in peace what we should do about them."

She translated. The old man made another speech, with the younger one chiming in, apparently in agreement. When they'd gotten it out of their systems, the girl said. "In that case, we are well met. We too were shot at by the strange *blancos* over that way. We have no idea why. Even when the pirates were there it was our custom to go over to the great salt water to hunt turtle eggs, and nobody ever bothered us. We are not evil people. It was wrong for them to chase us with their guns. Since they treated you the same way, the *brujo* says the spirits think you must not be evil people, either."

The old man started to rise. Captain Gringo said, "Wait! Where are you people going?"

She said, simply, "Back to our own camp, of course. We have found out you are not evil people and so we don't have to fight you. What else is there to say? I have heard of your strange god who is nailed to a cross of wood. That is how I learned your tongue. But I have never believed the story. It is not possible a god would allow himself to be treated in such an undignified manner. Even when the missionaries beat me, I refused to listen and, as you see, in time I got away."

"Wait, we're not missionaries. We respect whatever spirits you and your people would rather pray to. Tell the old one we have guns, many guns, and we would like to help you fight the men who frightened you!"

The old man was already walking off into the darkness. The younger one exchanged more gibberish with the girl as he stood above her, as if undecided about something. She rose, too. Lightly and gracefully. Those stocky but shapely legs had to be powerful, since she was no lightweight, despite her short stature. She said, "My brother, here, says he would like to fight the bad *blancos*. But he is an untested youth. The old ones know all too well what happens to *Indios* who fight *blancos*. I will tell them your words. I do not think they will wish to do anything. You are the only *blancos* near our home camp, and since you are not evil, what is the point in taking the warpath?"

He rose, too, saying, "I am called Dick. May I ask how you may be called, señorita?"

"I am not a señorita, I am not a silly *Cristiana*. My real name is my own secret, known only to close relations. If you wish, you may call me Decepcióna, for that is what the missionaries called me before I ran away."

Then she turned and walked off into the night without another word, with her brother following as silently.

Captain Gringo chuckled. A lot the missionaries knew when they nicknamed her Deception. She seemed to be one little gal who just plain spoke her mind. Like most Indians uncorrupted by so-called civilization, she probably never lied unless it was important. Indians weren't complete fools when it came to fibbing. Most would lie to save their asses. But they'd never picked up the charming habit of lying to be polite. It was too bad Queen Victoria never made that rule to go with all the other bullshit required in polite society these days!

Gaston had seen the Indians go. So he rejoined Captain Gringo to help smother the glowing coals with more damp duff. By the time Gaston was filled in, the others had come out, so Captain Gringo had to feed them a condensed version of the current situation, adding, "I don't think we'll have trouble with the Indians, and if anyone else we had to worry about was near enough to matter, the Indians would be long gone. The Mosquitoes have a rep as hit-and-run fighters."

"But they do fight?" asked Phoebe, fully dressed and looking like butter wouldn't melt in her mouth. He could play innocent too, so he nodded pleasantly and said, "Anyone fights if they have to, Miss Phoebe. The Mosquitoes don't make a habit of doing it for practice. Like I said, they're not bad guys if you leave 'em alone."

The grumpy Wilson growled, "We were never told there'd be wild red Indians! We've lost our proper leader without ever getting near the treasure trove, and I don't know about the rest of you, but I vote we pack it in while we still have our bonny scalps!"

Captain Gringo said, "Mosquito Indians don't scalp. They just put a poison arrow in you and run like hell. But you may have a point. Let's see a show of hands for turning back."

Nobody raised their hands except Wilson and Gaston. Captain Gringo said, "It's nice to see you two have made up. But you seem to be outvoted. Okay, gang, let's all head back to the sacks. There's still five or six hours of darkness left, and I warn you in advance you won't be able to kip out in those tents once it warms up again. Gaston, you may as well get some beauty rest too. I'll stand the next guard mount."

A few minutes later he was alone by the fire again. The fire no longer cast any visible light, so if anyone was planning on putting an arrow in him they'd have to wait until morning. He started walking, swinging out in a wide circle of the camp through the trees. It wasn't easy. He had to move slowly to keep from bumping his nose on a mahogany in the almost pitch darkness. But as his eyes got used to it, he could see maybe a few yards. Little spots of surprisingly bright sky glow filtered down through the overhead tree canopy. The moon had to be high as well as full. He couldn't see it. He hoped the compass on Sylvia's dash was accurate. He had this neck of the woods, he hoped, pinpointed on the map. But they were going to have to make a few more dog legs across the map through the unmapped jungle in the next day or so, and he really could have used an Indian guide, damn their uncaring shy souls.

He wondered what it would be like to lay chubby little Decepción. He wondered why he wondered. Phoebe had a nicer figure. Well, a different figure, anyway. Variety was the spice of life and Decepción was built as different from Phoebe as two dames could be built without one of 'em being a mess. He couldn't think of anything else he had to offer the Indian girl, and, aside from needing a guide, they might need a translator if they ran into another band less peacefully inclined, damn those other whites over to the east.

He wondered why the gang at the old pirate camp had chased the Indians off. If they had guns, big guns, they shouldn't have been worried about the fairly peaceful Mosquitoes attacking them. The cute little squaw had said her band used to get along with pirates, and that would have taken peaceful manners indeed.

The gang couldn't have been worried about the Indians beating them to the treasure. In the first place, jungle primitives had different values. If they wanted money badly enough to work at getting it, the banana plantations up and down the coast were hiring. In the second place, the Indians had had the area all to themselves for years after the Royal Navy cleaned out the pirate camp. Had they known or cared about whatever was there, they'd have taken it long ago.

He made it to Sylvia's Stanley and said to it, "They were afraid the Indians would gossip about something they're doing over by the big lagoon. Decepción a said missionaries pestered them from time to time."

He picked up the machine gun, adding, "I think we'd better move you inside the tent circle after all, pal. If some young buck decides to go joy riding in a steam car, we're out of luck. But they won't swipe you just for the hell of it."

He hefted the Maxim over one shoulder, wrapped it in its tarp, and took an ammo case in the other hand before trudging back inside the tent ring. He shoved it inside his tent. As he did so, a sleepy female voice murmured, "Who's there?"

He whispered, "Go back to sleep, doll," so she murmured, "All right," as he heard her turn over with a luxurious sigh of contentment. He smiled as he went back to walking the perimeter. For a gal who wanted to keep their affair so secret, Phoebe hadn't been thinking ahead. He'd have to make sure he woke Gaston while it was still dark. He knew they'd both want to tear off at least one more before he snuck her back to her own tent unseen by the others.

It didn't make his tour of guard duty go any faster, knowing there was a ready and willing little dame keeping his bed roll warm for him. But he forced himself to behave as he stayed alert, walking his post in a military manner, like the old general orders said, and sneaking a peek at his watch by matchlight until his supply of matches was in peril. Four hours by his watch and at least four months by his glands went by before he went to Gaston's tent, shook the flap, hard, and called out, "Rise and shine, old buddy. It's your turn to listen to the fucking crickets."

Gaston said a dreadful thing about his mother.

Captain Gringo said he had to stand guard anyway and moved on to his own tent, unbuckling his gun rig on the way. He ducked inside and knelt on the canvas flooring, listening to the soft breathing of the girl asleep in his bed roll as he quickly shucked his duds in the dark. He crawled in with her and gently rolled her over to press his nude flesh to hers. She protested mildly in her sleep, then started purring as he ran his hands over her to warm her up. He was warmed up pretty good, too. Thinking about the chunky short Indian girl had been a great notion, for Phoebe's body seemed bigger and leaner now. He wondered if he could get in without waking her. More than one playmate had told him in the past that she enjoyed waking up like that.

He rolled into her saddle, parted her genital lips with the head of his now raging erection, and slowly slid it into her relaxed warm opening. It contracted deliciously as he thrust all the way in and settled his weight gently on her cool breasts and belly. She spread her legs wider and thrust up to meet him with her hips as she murmured sleepily, "Oh, that feels so lovely." Then she woke up, gasped, and asked, "Who the fuck are *you*, and what are you doing in my fucking tent, and, my God, you seem to be fucking *me!*"

He gasped in surprise, too, as he recognized her voice. He asked, "Matilda?" and she snapped, "Who the flaming hell did you expect to find in my tent, Victoria Regina?"

"I'm not in your tent, dammit. You're in mine and, oops, I seem to be in you. Sorry."

He started to withdraw. She held him closer with her arms as she thrust her hips again and said, "For God's sake, don't stop now! Whoever you are, you have a lovely great dong! By the way, who are you?"

He grinned and said, "I don't think I'll tell you," as he proceeded to treat her right.

She laughed and said, "Oh, it has to be Captain Gringo. Nobody else in camp is this big, in every way, I see."

"Call me Dick, honey."

"I will if you'll dick me harder. Dear God, I'd almost forgotten how good it felt with a real man!"

She proved her point by doing more than half the work when she raised her knees to grip his ribs under the armpits as he dug his toes in and started long-donging her. He hadn't seen fit to comment on her remark about real men, but he saw now why she spent so much time away from home. She was built looser than Phoebe or, indeed, most women. It was good when she contracted, but her dilations were a little sloppy, even for him, and a man who wasn't hung right would have had to tie a board across his ass to keep from falling in. Her body, as he'd suspected from looking at her dressed more sedately, was lean and muscular. She was saved from being flat-chested, just, by a pair of small hard boobs that felt sort of like a boxer's biceps, save for the perky nipples rubbing against his chest as she rippled under him. She screwed like a man might have had he suddenly awakened with a vagina. Matilda was as earthy in bed with her body as she was the rest of the time with her mouth, God bless her. She minced no words as she said, "More, I want more! Fill me up and smooth out all the wrinkles of my cunt!"

He laughed and said, "I'm giving you my all, doll. Try biting down a little harder."

She did, and grasped his pumping shaft so hard it almost hurt as he ejaculated in her. She felt it and pleaded, "Don't stop! I'm almost there!" So he kept moving to be polite, but almost fell out when she gaped wide, contracted tightly, and shuddered in a long moaning climax before yawning again with her awesome love maw. He did drop out, then. He said, "Sorry," as he fumbled it back in her. There was more than room to spare, now. But if he kept his hips close to hers he could at least be courteous.

She said, "That was lovely. Do you think I have a big cunt?"

"Not when it matters. You'd know better than I if it's right for other guys. I know you may think it's none of my business, but have you been doing this with any of the others?"

"You mean the others on this boring expedition? Not bloody likely. I'm a married woman and they all belong to the same club as my twit of a husband. Besides, they're all a lot shorter than you. I've been terribly disappointed by more than one tall bloke, but at least, on the average, a man who's big one way can be expected to be big all over."

She tightened on him experimentally and added, "Hm, I see I haven't fatally injured you, but it does seem smaller now. Must be the added lubrication, what?"

He was too polite to agree as he started moving faster in her again. The novelty of her boyish body and the sheer perversity of the situation helped. He knew Phoebe wouldn't talk, but if she came in about now for a return match, the conversation promised to be grotesque. Matilda may have been thinking along the same lines. She said, "I say, we mustn't let the others know our little secret, Dick. As I said, same club, and *they'd* probably want some too."

"Mum's the word." He grinned, trying to come again but not having much luck with her so dilated. He said, "Uh, could you sort of bite down, honey?"

She did for a few strokes, and he was getting harder as she felt more reasonable between her long slim thighs. But she couldn't hold it all the way to heaven. As she heated up, her love box seemed to gasp for air every other stroke. It sounded vulgar, too, as trapped air farted against his nuts on the downstroke. It seemed to amuse her. She laughed and said, "I've never been able to control the damned thing once I've really warmed to the occasion. I know it's horrid. Fucking me must feel like fucking a great cow, but I can't help it. I say, are you game for something a bit unusual, Dick?"

He didn't think they ought to go sixty-nine. He hadn't bathed since he'd been in another woman earlier that night, and it didn't seem decent to have Matilda inhale him, even though her big mouth had to be tighter. He knew she hadn't been with anyone recently, so what the hell. He said, "I'm game for anything that doesn't hurt. What did you have in mind?"

She said, "Let me up. I have to get on top to do it." So he rolled out of the saddle and lay on his back, still semierect but not half as hot as he'd started. Once the novelty wore off, he had to admit that Phoebe had been a better lay, damn her discreet little snatch. He realized, now, that Phoebe had packed it in and was sleeping in her own tent. Matilda had crawled into the wrong one in the dark. Swell. So how was he to get rid of her without hurting her feelings?

He expected her to go down on him and was braced to return the favor in kind, as a good host should. But to his mild surprise she forked a leg across him to squat on her heels, facing him, as she reached down and gathered his privates in both hands, balls and all. As she lowered her widespread groin against the love bundle she was holding in her hands, she explained, "I can't do this unless I almost do a split. But, with a little bit of luck . . ."

He laughed as he caught on and said, "It won't work, doll. There's not a man who hasn't tried it. But it still won't work. Balls-and-all is just a pool-hall brag."

Then he gasped as he felt her inhaling with her internal muscles, and as she settled her full weight against his pelvis he marveled, "Jesus, you're amazing. For God's sake, don't clamp down now!"

She started moving up and down with his scrotum and suddenly inspired shaft enveloped in her pulsating warm wetness as she cooed, "Oh, that does feel tight. Do you like it, Dick?"

"I think so. It feels sort of weird. Could you move a little faster?"

She gingerly lowered her knees to the sheet on either side of his hips as she pressed down firmly and said, "Not without ruining you for life or, even worse, losing your lovely balls."

She braced herself with one hand on his chest as she leaned forward, crotch gaping and well filled as she began to play with her own clit with her other hand. It wasn't doing a hell of a lot for him. It just teased the hell out of him to have everything he owned in a sack of warm jelly as she gripped tighter with the opening around the roots of everything and jerked her crazy self off. He tried to join the fun by thrusting up and down with his own hips. But she was heavy and rode with it, so he just added to the frustration as he learned, the hard way, that balls and all was more confusion than fun.

But Matilda sure liked it. She moaned in animal pleasure as she strummed her clit like a banjo and enjoyed a long lingering orgasm with her unfortunately proportioned snatch fully packed for a change. The results were more painful for him.

He hissed, "Jeeeezusss!" as she tightened internally, gripping his genitals in a vise of warm wet velvet. It made him hard as a high-school boy in a whorehouse, but he couldn't move enough to come with her.

She relaxed her hold on him and slid off him with a loud wet pop. He didn't care if she was satisfied or not. He was stiff as a poker and wanted to come again, even if he had to wag it like a dog's tail to touch both sides.

He propped himself up on one elbow, meaning to remount her as soon as she lay back down. But Matilda was still full of frisky tricks. She slid down him to take his raging erection between her pursed lips, and as she swallowed his shaft beyond her tonsils he exploded in her mouth almost at once. She didn't spit anything out. She gulped and kept sucking as she moved her own lap into position above his face. He took a deep breath and prepared to be a good sport. She smelled clean, at least, and nobody but himself had come in her in recent memory. But as he started to tease her clit with the tip of his tongue, she came up for air long enough to say, "I'm too sensitive there! Fuck me with your fist!"

That sure beat shoving a tongue up her snatch, if it would work. He knew she was built big, but this was ridiculous. Captain Gringo had big hands.

It was her idea, though. So as she drove him nuts with her skilled lips and remarkable gag control, he slid four fingers in, saw he could get the thumb in with a little effort, and then he was in her to the wrist with his fingers clenched in a fist, the knuckles against her cervix. She must have liked it. She started wagging her ass from side to side, rubbing the mouth of her womb over his knuckles as she clamped down on the head of his excited organ with her throat muscles and began literally to screw him with her head, lips tightly pursed around the base of his shaft as she alternately swallowed and half-retched until they came together.

It damned near cracked his knuckles, and he thought his balls were going to get sucked up inside her mouth.

He lay limp as a dish rag as she crawled around to lay her head on his shoulder, murmuring, "God, to think I might have wound up finding my own bloody tent. We're going to have to be careful, darling, but I'm glad we found each other at last."

He didn't answer. Freak shows were all right for a change of pace. But now that the bloom was off the lily, what the hell was he supposed to do about the other sneaky arrangement he had with Phoebe? Matilda would probably go for three in a boat. But he'd promised them both he wouldn't tell anyone else, and Phoebe seemed a little old-fashioned, as well as a better lay.

Matilda said, "I suppose I should be thinking of getting back to my own chaste bed before it gets too light out. But I'm still hot. How about you?"

"I'd like to do it again," he lied, "but we'd better not take chances. It must be close to five, and the sun comes up like thunder at six in the tropics. Dawns are boring as hell down here. You can set your watch by 'em."

He held her closer and kissed her, meaning it as a gentle dismissal. She didn't take it that way. She said, "We've time for one last quicky, Dick," and rolled up on her hands and knees, adding, "Doggy-style is a good way to do it fast, don't you agree?"

He had his reservations about that. Mounting from behind was a good if unromantic way to break a virgin in, since it opened a woman well. But if there was one thing Matilda didn't need, it was to be opened wider.

But what the hell, he could get it in half-soft in that position and he didn't want to send her home unhappy. So he got behind her on his own knees, grabbed a hip bone, and fumbled it in. She said, "Either I'm getting looser or you're getting smaller. We seem to have started an exercise in futility, dear."

"I noticed. Why don't we call it a night?"

"I'm about satisfied for now, but I don't want to leave you frustrated, now that you've started, darling."

"Oh, I can always jerk off."

"Why waste it? I know, shove it up my bum."

That sounded like a good idea. He was coming to life down there again and he didn't have to worry about hurting a woman built so slackly between the hips. Most girls found him a bit much for Greek loving, so that offered another novelty, too. He got the slippery tip in place above her grand canyon and thrust against the involuntary resistance of her anal muscles until it suddenly popped in. Matilda hissed, "Oooooh, Jesus, you do have a big one!"

He was pleasantly surprised, too. Matilda's back door was tighter than expected. Tighter than most he'd been in, as a matter of fact. He guessed nature had to take up the slack somewhere. He asked, "Am I hurting you?" and she said, "A little, but don't stop. I love the feeling of fullness in me." So he held a hip bone in each hand and started moving faster as she arched her spine to take it deep while she strummed her clit some more.

He knew he'd feel ashamed of himself in the cold gray light of dawn. But it wasn't dawn yet, and she really took it great in the brown. She must have been telling the truth about liking it that way, for she came just ahead of him, groaning in pleasure as she rubbed her firm buttocks hard against his pelvis until he ejaculated in her and they both fell weakly on their sides, with her spooned in his lap until she slowly defecated him in a series of throbbing mock bowel movements. He kissed the nape of her neck. She said, "That's enough. I have to take a shit and get back to my tent."

So as long as she'd put it so delicately, he let her go. She left still nude, scooping up her clothes on the way as she told him not to make any overt moves in public, adding that she'd let him know when the time was right again.

He sat up, groped for a kerchief and canteen in the dark, and cleaned himself before hauling on his pants and boots. There was no sense trying to sleep now. The night was shot and he was wide awake, if bone weary. At least the coming day should be a lazy one. They couldn't move from here just yet, and when they did, he'd get to ride. Driving through the jungle in steam cars sounded crazy, until one considered the alternatives. Meanwhile, he'd get up and relieve Gaston. He'd been treated mighty generously for one night, so he felt in a generous mood.

He finished dressing, strapped on his .38, but left his hat and jacket behind as he stepped out to scout up Gaston. It was still pretty dark, but you could see movement now. Gaston did and challenged him. He said. "It's me. How's it going? See anything?"

*"Merde alors,* I can barely make you out. One of the women just went out past the cars to take la crap. I was about to challenge her when I heard her squat and drop it, so I didn't. Before you ask, only a woman squats when she makes la pee-pee, so . . ."

"Never mind. I know who it was. I was talking about our Indian chums."

"I would have called you had anyone shot an arrow at me. They are probably moving deeper into the jungle. We make *them très* nervous, too."

Then, as they stood close together, Gaston said, "Listen! I hear something making le crunch-crunch in the dead leaves out to the east!"

Captain Gringo heard it too. He frowned and said, "Someone's started one of the steam cars! What the hell . . . ?"

"What the hell indeed! No Indian would know how, and this is a most unusual time to be going for a drive, *non?*"

They both started moving toward the sound, guns drawn and ready for anything, they thought. But the last thing they'd expected was for a steam car to roll into camp, flattening Captain Gringo's tent as it rolled on majestically with nobody behind the wheel!

The tall American ran over to it as Gaston moved the other way to see who'd started it out in the surrounding darkness. Captain Gringo leaped aboard the slow-moving car and shut the throttle before grabbing the emergency brake to stop it. Then he saw that that hadn't been such a good move as he smelled burning rubber. He'd stopped with the front wheels on the banked campfire! He swung behind the steering wheel, threw the steamer in reverse, and backed off the hot coals before stopping again more easily on the rolling stock. The tires were still smoking and stank like hell, but they were solid rubber, so no great damage had been done, he hoped.

The noise of crunching tent poles and snapping ropes had aroused some of the others. As Gaston rejoined him, muttering, "Nothing," Bertie and the surly Wilson came over, asking what had happened.

He saw they were both half-undressed and supposed it took longer for the women and more modest men to rise and shine. He said, "Some silly son of a bitch started this car up just now. It's the one you've been driving since Wallace bought it, Bertie."

"By Jove, so it is! But this makes no sense, captain. Steam cars don't start by accident, you know!"

"I know. Ergo, it was no accident. I know you never left the flame on under the boiler. I passed your parked car a million times in the dark, earlier tonight. It wasn't parked facing my tent, either. Some son of a bitch aimed it at me, then jumped off after leaving the hand throttle set slow but sure. Lucky for me I'm an early riser!"

Bertie gasped. "Good God, are you saying someone tried to *murder* you? I'd best say right off I was in the tent I share with Jerome and, ah, here comes Jerome now!"

As the little Welshman approached, tucking in his shirt tail and gulping his Adam's apple as usual, Bertie said, "Some blighter just tried to run over our Yank. Tell him where we were, like a good Taffy lad, Jerome!"

Jerome gulped and said, "I was in the tent with you when the noise woke me, look you. But what's this about someone being run over? I don't see anyone run over, do you?"

Captain Gringo left them to sort it out as he went to survey the damages. Gaston followed, murmuring, "I agree a man would have to be a bigger fool even than they to use his own vehicle. That leaves us with enough suspects to go around, *non?*"

Captain Gringo didn't answer as he hauled aside the flattened tent and whistled. The heavy wheels had left tracks in the canvas ground cloth by pressing it into the soft soil below. One wheel had gone right across his sleeping bag. The other had flattened his sombrero. He picked it up, punched it back into shape, and put it on, observing, "I'm glad my head wasn't in it at the time!"

Others were coming on in the slowly dawning light as Gaston murmured, "Let me see, there are Baxter, Gordon, and Fenton, in addition to the four women, and hell hath no fury like . . . have you been scorning any women lately, Dick?"

"Scorning isn't the word I'd have chosen. Knock it off. The others are coming and we've known all along that at least two of them figure to be sneaks."

Considering how exciting the night had been, the day that followed was dull as hell. Captain Gringo told the others it was too soon to move on the old pirate camp blindly. Before they dared even to scout it, they had to give the other side time to assume the English expedition had given up.

He didn't give his other reason for delay. Why alert the guilty party or parties to the fact that he was watching for someone to make a slip?

As they helped him put his tent back together, using fresh-cut poles from the jungle and splicing some of the lines, one of the men suggested that an Indian prankster might have been fooling with Bertie's steam car, so Captain Gringo pretended to accept the explanation, even knowing that not one *white* kid in a hundred knew how to start a horseless carriage.

As the women made breakfast, or stood around helpfully as, in fact, Sylvia and Pat did most of the work, both Phoebe and Matilda seemed content to keep the little secret each thought she shared alone with Captain Gringo, although both wore funny little Mona Lisa smiles from time to time as they puttered about.

Breakfast came and went. Then they had lunch, and as the day grew even warmer Captain Gringo decreed a siesta, explaining, "I know none of you lime juicers are used to the custom, but get used to it. There's nothing to do out here but soak up rays from the canopy above us that won't do you a bit of good. Try to get some sleep, despite the hour. You never know when you'll be called upon to stay awake in this game. Bertie, I'm putting you on guard duty until two. Get Jerome here to take your place until four, then wake everybody up. I'll be in my tent if you need me, but don't, unless it's important as hell. For some reason I feel beat."

Matilda laughed and turned away and almost ran to her own tent. But nobody commented. They were used to the big gal's odd ways. Phoebe was examining her nails as if they needed a lot of work when he passed her on his way to his tent. He hoped she wouldn't follow. He really needed a couple of hours' sleep.

He took off his shirt and gun, tossed his hat in a corner, and lay atop the bed-roll covers with his pants and boots still on, in case.

He closed his eyes and was half-asleep when the tent flap opened and a feminine voice whispered, "Are you awake?"

He groaned and said, "I am now. No shit, doll, I'm too tired to fuck."

"What a beastly suggestion!" She gasped.

So he opened his eyes to see Sylvia kneeling there at his side. He propped himself up on one elbow and said, "Forget what I just said."

"I don't see how I can! I'm not accustomed to being spoken to that way, sir!"

He sighed again and said, "Yeah, yeah, us Yanks have no couth. If you didn't like my first offer, what the hell *do* you want? I'm really tired, Sylvia."

She said, "Well, so am I, dammit, and I can't sleep in my own bloody tent. Do you know what Pat and that nasty little French friend of yours are doing over there this very minute?"

"I can guess. I know Gaston of old, and you told me the redhead's warm-natured too."

He eyed her thoughtfully in the shady light. Sylvia's knees were sedately folded under her, covered by her skirt. But she'd either left her tent in a hurry or she was trying to tell him something. The front of her blouse wasn't buttoned and that V of exposed flesh between her nicely formed breasts sure looked nice. He still liked her face, despite the dumb things that came out of it. From the beginning she'd been the best-looking dish in the stack, and he couldn't complain about Phoebe's or Matilda's looks. But, Jesus, was he man enough, on such short notice?

He patted the bedding at his side and said, "You're welcome to stay here during *la siesta,* if that was what you had in mind."

"Not bloody likely! Gaston already suggested making it a beastly orgy. That's what I came to see you about. You have to have a talk with Gaston."

"Why? Cat's got Pat's tongue? I doubt like hell they want to be disturbed right now, Sylvia. I don't think Gaston meant two guys and a gal when he suggested three in a boat. It's more fun the other way, at least for guys."

"Oh, God, you're just impossible!"

"Nobody's impossible, honey. Maybe I'm a little improbable. You're cute as hell, and someday I'll kick myself, but if all you want is a place to spend your siesta, lie down and shut up, for God's sake. I had a hard night. I'm going to sleep no matter what you do."

He lay back down and closed his eyes. Sylvia hesitated, then asked, "Can I trust you, Dick?"

"To do what? I told you it was your show, dammit. Lie down for a nap or go out and chin yourself on a tree, for all I care."

"You won't . . . take advantage of me?"

"Oh, shit, why do the pretty ones always have to come with no brains? If you thought I'd rape you, why the hell did you creep into my tent like a love-sick Arab? Don't tell me. I'm too tired for dumb conversations. I'm going to sleep. You do whatever you want to."

There was a long silence. Then she said, "I think you might be a true gentleman, despite your rough talk, and I certainly have no place else to spend the siesta. Ah, is it all right if I slip off my outer garments? It's so perishing hot and stuffy in here. I'm wearing my unmentionables, of course."

"Don't mention them, then, and for chrissake shut up! Every time I start to fall asleep you ask another dumb question!"

It took even longer for her to slip out of her heavy whipcord skirt, if that was the rustle he heard. He didn't open his eyes. She whispered, "Dick?" and he didn't answer. If he played possom just a little longer, she'd be on the roll with him and . . . then what? He was too tired to wrestle, and he'd met dames like this one before. He knew she halfway wanted it, whether she admitted it to herself or not. The trouble with halfway dames was that they always sobbed that you were raping them while they seduced you.

She slid gingerly in place beside him on the padding. He didn't move. Two could play at teasing, and he was really too tired to be teased. The hell with it. She'd asked him not to, right?

When he woke up a couple of hours later, Sylvia was snuggled like a kitten against him, asleep herself, unless she was one hell of an actress with mighty calm nerves. She'd come to bed in her blouse and loose silk pantaloons, as she'd promised, but one long silk-sheathed leg lay across his thighs and she had her pubic mound pressed against his hip for comfort.

Her blouse had fallen open and he'd been right about her having great boobs. One, at least. He couldn't see them both, as the bottom one was pressed against his rib cage. Somehow they'd wound up with her head on his shoulder with his right arm cradling her against him, so some of it wasn't her fault, and she was going to be surprised one way or another if and when she woke up in that position. He decided not to. He didn't like to hear screaming dames even when he *had* laid them. He lay quietly, trying to decide why he had awakened. Thanks to good old Phoebe and crazy Matilda, he didn't have a hard-on. He must have heard something. But he didn't hear anything now, did he? Yeah, someone was scuffing the damp leaves outside. The tent flap opened and Gaston said, *"Eh bien,* Pat *said* she liked you!"

Sylvia woke with a start, gasped, and, as she realized what she'd been rubbing her snatch against in that dream, started to say something dumb. But Gaston said, "Later, M'mselle. This is not time for a lover's spat. Those Indians have returned. I think they prefer to speak to you, Dick!"

Captain Gringo sat up as Sylvia rolled out of the way, crossing her legs and covering her chest with both hands. As he strapped on his .38 over his virile bare chest, she asked him, "Did you? Did we?" and he said, "For God's sake, you've still got your pants on. Better put some other stuff on before you come out, though. It's still broad day outside."

He followed Gaston over to the fire, where the same two Indian men and the girl hunkered alone. They looked even nuder in the daylight, and he could see, now, that Decepcióna's snatch was shaved, not immature. The other whites had been smart enough to stay out of sight as told the last time. Doubtless they were watching from their tents, of course, as Captain Gringo sat on his haunches and silently handed the cigar he'd brought out to the old man.

The *brujo* ignored it as he gonged and whimpered in his mysterious lingo. Captain Gringo thought they might be in trouble, until the Spanish-speaking squaw explained, "There is no time for ceremony. We came to tell you the evil men who chased us from the great salt water and our turtle grounds are coming this way, with guns, many guns. The *brujo* says to tell you our scouts counted thirty of them."

"Are you sure they're not after *your* people, Decepcióna? There's no way they could know we're here!"

"They are not making for our camp. They are coming here in the line of the honey bee. One of them has a little box he keeps looking at. It seems to be a medicine fetish with a spirit in it to point the way."

Gaston, who'd just decided it was all right to squat down beside Captain Gringo, murmured, "Compass. The species of triple-titted toads are running a compass azimuth through jungle we could not have left tracks in! Ergo, they have us on their own map! But that is not possible!"

He'd spoken in Spanish to be polite, so Decepcióna had followed enough to chime in, "Hear me, they will be here before dark whether it is possible or not. The *brujo*, here, has been speaking with our other elders. He says you seem to be good people. He says you should come to our camp, where our own spirits are strong. The spirits in the bad *blancos'* medicine box will not be able to find you there."

In a way, she was probably right. If the other side had an azimuth reading on this area, some damned how, they'd miss a camp well to the north or south.

He asked the girl exactly how far the armed men were. Decepcióna said, "Less than two hours, as you people tell time. The *brujo* here says if you do not hurry, we must leave without you. His medicine is not good here. He is afraid of those other *blancos*."

Captain Gringo nodded, turned to Gaston, and said, "Okay, get everybody saddled up and move 'em out, segundo. You heard the lady say less than two hours, and you'll want at least an hour's lead on them. That gives you fifteen minutes to strike the tents and load the cars up. Oh, tell Bertie to start all the boiler fires right away, so you'll have steam up when you're set to go!"

"Dick, those four heavy cars will leave tracks."

"You just figured that out? Let's get cracking. I have to set up a machine-gun ambush while you pack!"

"You're staying behind alone?"

"Move your ass, you old windbag!" snapped Captain Gringo. So Gaston did, as the American explained to the Indians about the steam cars being good medicine that their spirits should get along with just fine.

An hour or so later he was feeling mighty lonely. It was still daylight, praise God, from whom all blessings flow, but he was pretty sure nobody would spot his spider hole in time to do them any good. He'd used a spade from the supplies to dig an oversized trapdoor spider nest in the red clay under the forest duff. He'd chosen the spot with care, so he could toss the red spoil over a fallen log, out of sight, and the log at his back would make it harder to spot his head when he had to pop up. At the moment he was down in the hole on his butt, with the Maxim on his thighs and the ammo canister between his boot heels. It made for a snug fit, but he hadn't had time to excavate a cellar. He'd pulled dead branches over his hole, but arched them enough that he could peek over the rim without moving them. His field of fire was of course the recently vacated camp. There was nothing there now but the artistically burning fire. He didn't want the other side to get lost. The rising smoke would be visible quite a distance in the cathedrallike gloom between the massive gray tree trunks, if they were looking hard enough to worry about.

He saw movement beyond the fire. Had an advance scout made it past him to circle in from that direction? Pretty slick. But now the jerk-off would call the others and . . . Shit, it was Gaston.

The little Frenchman came closer to the fire with his Winchester held at port across his chest as he looked around, sincerely bewildered, until Captain Gringo yelled, "Over here, on the double, you snail-eating asshole!"

Gaston trotted his way but didn't spot him until Captain Gringo said, "Oh, hell," and moved the branches above him.

Gaston stiffened, dropped into a gunfighter's crouch with the Winchester trained his way, and called out, "Is that you, Dick?"

"If I was anyone else you'd be dead. What the fuck are you doing here?"

"I was lonely. I got all the others to the Indian camp a long time ago and ran back to see if you needed help."

"I don't. There's not room in this hole for the two of us."

"Ah, I see the plan. *Très pratique. Eh bien*, I shall hide my adorable ass behind the log in back of you, *non?*"

"*No*, dammit! I dug in here because I wanted to keep some son of a bitch from walking up behind me and stepping on my head by accident. Nobody should climb over that log behind me when there are so many easier ways to go, but if anyone approaches from the other side, *your* adorable ass will make an adorable target. Start back to the Indian camp on the double. I don't need a guide. I'll follow the tracks."

Gaston nodded but said, "Too late!" and dived over the big log out of sight. Captain Gringo had heard them too. They were coming down their compass heading like big-ass birds with the self-confident swagger of the armed and dangerous bully boy.

He grimaced in distaste and checked his Maxim's action again. There was nothing to do but pull the trigger of the loaded and primed machine gun, but a guy wanted to be sure. He knew Gaston was as tense or tenser right now, but, unlike the gang coming their way, neither soldier of fortune made a habit of loud conversation while moving in on an objective.

Jesus Christ, they were a noisy bunch. Could that be a ruse? Any scouts they had out ahead would be walking tippy-toe, and the shouted military commands off to the east could be a ploy to distract. But he didn't see said scouts, and, as the loud voices got nearer, he could tell that some officer or noncom was trying to keep his men in a neat skirmish line as they moved through the trees. He'd noticed that that first bunch had been lined up like soldiers on parade, too. He grinned wolfishly as he crouched in his hole. Please, God, let them pass in file on parade so he could mow 'em down like chumps!

They almost did. As he spotted the long line of riflemen coming through the trees from the east, a burly figure was running up and down the line like a platoon sergeant trying to keep them properly dressed down to pass in review.

They weren't dressed like soldiers. Like the first bunch, they wore ragged peon disguises, but that wasn't Spanish their leader was shouting. It wasn't English, either. What the fuck was going on? Nobody but native troops or the U.S. Marines were allowed down here in Honduras. It said so, right in the Monroe Doctrine.

One of them spotted the rising smoke and brought it to their leader's attention. He called a halt and sent two men forward to investigate. Captain Gringo let them pass. He knew what they'd find. He'd wanted them to.

They circled the campfire, one of them kicked at it for some dumb reason, then they waved the others in to the deserted camp.

They didn't get there. As the skirmish line swept past Captain Gringo's position, a little ragged, damn them, he stood up with the Maxim braced against his hip and opened up on them full automatic!

He cut half of them down with his first long burst, then hosed left and right to polish off the ones who hadn't been lined up as their leader wanted them. Behind him, Gaston was banging away with his Winchester, for some reason. What was Gaston up to? Oh, yeah, the two guys by the fire. Nice going, Gaston.

He still had a quarter of the first belt left when he ceased fire for lack of moving targets. He rested the Maxim on the edge of the hole to climb out as Gaston's rifle spanged again. He called out, "Dammit, Gaston, don't finish off any wounded until I have a chat with them!"

Gaston rose from behind the log to reply, "I was not shooting at anyone on your side of the log, my hasty child. An odd little man in a straw hat was moving in behind you with one of those adorable new Krag rifles."

"I stand corrected. Cover me while I have a look at what we just bagged."

He drew his .38 to approach the first downed enemy he came to. The guy wasn't ever going to be a threat to anyone, ever again. The bastard didn't have a bit of I.D. on him, either. Just pocket change and an ammo bandoleer. The others all seemed to be playing dead Mexican bandits, too. But they were a little too far south, and that was not Mexican they'd been yelling as he'd mowed them down.

He saw he was wasting time on the enlisted scum. He moved over to the husky leader, sprawled face down in the dirt with his face in his hat like a horse eating oats. He rolled the slob over, saw that the hat was stuck to his face with blood and brains, and said, "Well, since you're not in a mood to talk, let's see what you have in your pockets."

There was no I.D. By now he'd learned not to expect it. Whoever had sent these guys out into the jungle didn't want them identified when they lost. That sounded reasonable.

He found a pocket compass. That was no surprise. Then he found something that was. The Indians had been right about it being a black box. The leader had a set of earphones and a little crystal Marconi receiver under his shirt!

Captain Gringo holstered his .38, put one earphone to his head, and fiddled with the cat's whisker on the rough germanium crystal without picking up anything except what sounded like someone frying bacon somewhere. He went back to join Gaston. As he stepped over the log he spotted another white-clad corpse face down in the distance. He nodded and said, "Thanks. Look what I found, mother."

Gaston took the crystal set and said, *"Très* interesting toy to find on a mere guerrilla, *non?"*

"Hell, we've known all along they were some kind of military outfit. If I'm up on the state of the art, you can send those radio waves twenty or thirty miles, tops. Marconi keeps bragging that someday he'll be able to send them across the ocean, but so far he can't seem to do it."

"*Oui,* we should be within sending range of their base camp over by the lagoon. Could they talk back with this thing?"

"No way; a Marconi sending set is too heavy for two men to carry."

"*Eh bien,* in that case, base has no way of knowing this patrol was not such a grand idea after all. If we buried this garbage . . ."

"Forget it. Aside from it being too much work in this heat, they were following an azimuth this far, so any pals sent to look for 'em would find 'em in time no matter how deep we planted 'em. What I'm trying to figure is how they lined up on us, here, from back there!"

"Perhaps with that amusing electrical device?"

"I don't see how. They could take a bearing on the transmitter with this crystal set. But it wouldn't shoot a beam our way unless someone knew which way to aim it. Just following the compass works as well, and it's a lot less complicated."

Gaston started to toss the crystal set away. Captain Gringo grabbed it and snapped, "Are you nuts?"

"*Mais non,* just tired of carrying useless baggage. What good is that toy to us, Dick?"

"Jesus, you're dumb! We just agreed it'll take hours, probably all night, before they find their lost patrol. Meanwhile, they may send further instructions to them, see?"

"Perhaps, but do you speak German?"

"No. Is that what that was?"

"Of course. No Frenchman would ever mistake a Boche for a Dutchman or a Swede. Obviously, dear little Kaiser Willy is up to something *très dramatique* in this part of the world again. He never seems to learn. But, as I just asked, do you speak German? I know a few words, but not enough to listen in on their radio conversations."

Captain Gringo pocketed the set, nodded, and stepped over the log to get his machine gun as he growled, "Don't worry about it. I'm beginning to think someone in our party might.

Let's get back to them pronto. Don't mention this crystal set, and we'd better leave the details of what just happened here sort of fuzzy, too."

"I understand, to a point. But why are we going back to them, now that we know?"

"Know what? Who the spy or spies among us might be? I haven't a clue."

"Dick, now it is *you* who are not thinking. We have been had by that damned British Intelligence again! Can't you see it? The last time we worked for Greystoke you told him we'd never work for him again, *non?*"

"Right; the cheap bastard tends to use people as disposable pawns, and when they live through one of his deals, he tends to welsh on paying the agreed price."

"I was there. On the other hand, Greystoke knows you and I are the best in the business. He sent that girl to seduce you into joining this so-called treasure hunt because his agents, the so-called silly English people we've been guarding with our lives, needed a machine gunner who thinks fast on his feet. Why are you still following the car tracks? Did you not hear a word I just said?"

"Sure I did. Some of it makes sense. Major Wallace works as a British agent. Marlowe works as a German plant who blew up when he thought we knew more than we really did. Some of the others could be dupes, even as you and I. Meanwhile, we're miles from anywhere, without provisions for a lonely cross-country romp, and night's coming on."

"*Eh bien*, we go on to the Indian camp. We load up one of the steam cars with goodies—perhaps Pat and Sylvia, if they don't speak German—and then it's off to Patuca and a beautiful pea-green boat before either the British spies or the German spies mop our poor bewildered asses, *non?*"

Captain Gringo trudged on in silence as he considered all their options. Then he said, "When you're right you're right, Gaston. I don't like Kaiser Willy but I don't like being used and abused, repeat abused. I don't think we'll bother taking the dames along, though. A guy with a spiffy Stanley Steamer can always pick up a dame, and even if we can trust 'em, they'll slow us down, and what will we do with 'em after?"

"Don't you trust Sylvia? I don't think Pat could be a German or a British spy. Either job would call for more brains than she has. And I thought you and Sylvia were getting along quite nicely when I walked in on you."

"Oh, well, maybe we can take them along if they're awfully good."

The sun went down like it came up in the tropics, with no screwing around, and it was pretty gloomy under a rain-forest canopy even at high noon. So it was pitch black when they made it to the Indian village. Captain Gringo would have had trouble finding it after he couldn't see the tire tracks, had not Gaston already known the general direction.

Naturally they were spotted by an Indian scout long before they saw the glow of night fires ahead. So as they walked into the village there was a multiracial welcoming committee waiting for them by the main fire between the thatched huts.

The village was fairly substantial, for, despite their sensible costume in a hot climate, the Mosquito Indians were slash-and-burn agriculturists. They had no defensive stockade around the village, but the Indians' best defense was building villages that were not easy to find. There were no corn milpas near the village. They cleared and cultivated patches at least two miles away from their women and children as a simple but effective military strategy. So the village was surrounded by virgin jungle.

The old *brujo* and a younger man with lots of feathers made welcoming speeches that the cute squaw, Decepcióna, had to translate. They were so long and pointless they even bored her.

Captain Gringo half-listened as he exchanged nods with the whites in his party, watching over the heads of the short squat Indians.

Gaston had already told him that the steam cars were parked well out in the trees to the northwest of the village in order to avoid crowding the small spaces between the huts and to ensure a logical escape route if they had to leave in a hurry. Since Indian kids swiped things as quickly as any others, the supplies had been stored in one of the huts the Indians had provided for the expedition's use. No tents had been pitched. That would have been rude, whether the whites liked sleeping in the hammocks the young chief had offered or not.

The head men finally ran out of things to say and Decepcióna told them it was okay if they joined the other whites for supper. So they did.

The expedition had been issued its own neighborhood at the north end of the village of perhaps thirty families. As soon as the Indians backed off politely to let the whites sip tea and talk around their own night fire, Captain Gringo looked around and asked Bertie, "Where is everybody? We seem to be missing some faces."

Bertie said, "Not only that, we're missing a perishing steam car! I don't know when it happened. But apparently Fenton, Gordon, and Matilda have had enough. They took off in the White that Gordon's been driving!"

Captain Gringo started to rise, then settled back as he realized it was pointless to chase steam cars with a good lead in the dark. As Phoebe handed him a plate of beans and a secretive wink, he stared morosely across the fire, counting noses. They still had three steam cars. So, let's see, he had seats for Gaston and himself, Sylvia, Pat, Phoebe, Bertie, the sullen Wilson, and the gulping Jerome. Who was driving what? They'd been reshuffling the steering wheels since starting out and, okay, he had enough drivers and maybe enough fuel oil.

Wilson apparently had been thinking along the same lines. He scowled into the flames as he said, "I don't see what could have possessed them. When we saw they'd driven off, I ran to check our reserve kerosene tins and they didn't steal any."

Jerome gulped and said, "They'll never make it back to Puerto Cabezas on what they had in Gordon's steamer, look you! I never thought much of Gordon's brains, and Fenton is no genius. But I thought Lady Matilda had more sense."

Phoebe, sitting by Captain Gringo rather possessively, said, "They're sure to wind up stuck in the jungle somewhere and I must say it serves them bloody right!"

Captain Gringo ate his beans and thought before he spoke. He had a pretty good idea why Matilda had cut out, poor cow. It hadn't been Gordon's or Fenton's idea to take her along. She'd probably seen them firing up the boiler and insisted on going along.

By now she knew that he was wise to why she'd aimed that steam car right at the tent she'd just laid him in. A married lady with a reputation that meant more to her than her husband had had second thoughts after recovering her mind. It hadn't mattered that he'd promised not to kiss and tell. Ever so veddy-veddy English ladies simply did not take it in the arse from uncouth knock-around guys who'd never been to the right schools.

He finished his plate as the others speculated on the fate of their missing members. Some of the speculation was pretty dumb. He washed down the beans with a cup of pretty good tea, whoever'd brewed it, and turned to Gaston to say, "I think it's cards-on-the-table time. Now that we seem to have separated the wheat from the chaff, what say we take 'em all with us?"

Gaston shrugged and said, *"Oui,* if they'll go. I have never been able to decide whether English or German species of idiots are more stubborn."

Bertie frowned and growled, "Oh, I say, you bloody little Frog!"

Captain Gringo said, "Relax. He meant it as a compliment. He compliments my mother regularly."

Then, as they all stared at him in the flickering light, Captain Gringo raised his voice slightly to be heard by all present as he said, "Okay, gang, the party's over. Matilda just left because she's, ah, impulsive. I think Gordon and Fenton just showed their hand, and it's a good thing for you they decided to do it the easy way. The original plan was probably to kill you poor innocent dupes. Wallace was working for Der Kaiser. We just found out that the guys so interested in holding Laguna Caratasca against all comers are square heads. Probably German marines. Fenton and Gordon were with Wallace. You kiddies, and Gaston and I, were camouflage. Both Nicaraguan and Honduran authorities tend to accept the fact that adventurous Brits do all sorts of things too nutty to worry much about, so . . ."

"That's crazy!" cut in Pat, of all people. The redhead dimpled at Gaston as she added, "Gaston said that remittance man, Marlowe, was the secret agent who killed poor Major Wallace!"

"Gaston was wrong. So was I. Marlowe was either a British agent or a patriotic bum who'd caught on. He tried to keep Wallace from reaching the German base and, as a last resort, went down fighting for the Union Jack."

Bertie gasped. "My God! I was the one who shot Marlowe!"

"Don't feel bad about it. Marlowe wasn't waving the Union Jack at you at the time. He couldn't take anyone else into his confidence, because he couldn't know who was a German agent and who was just a jerk-off, no offense."

Wilson grumbled, "You certainly seem to know a lot, of a sudden, Yank. Who told you all this muck about German bases and Wallace being a German spy? Dammit, we belonged to the same club, and *I'm* no bloody German spy!"

"Lots of people belong to the same clubs. Your Prince of Wales owns stock in Krupp of Essen and Der Kaiser is his cousin. Wallace may not have considered himself a traitor to

Great Britain. Only a few people in the British Intelligence community are worried about the way Kaiser Willy seems to be preparing for one hell of a war with someone. A lot of perfectly decent Brits are betting on it being Russia, so they don't care."

Wilson shrugged and said, "Get to the point, man! It looks to me as if Wallace must have been working for British Intelligence if he was working for anyone!"

Bertie said, "He's right, you know. Mayhaps Wallace used us with that tale of buried pirate treasure. But have you forgotten those German chaps waiting to ambush us back at the river?"

Captain Gringo said, "They weren't waiting to ambush Wallace or his confederates. They were a *welcoming committee!* That's why they hadn't taken basic precautions despite obviously being trained marines. Marlowe was the only one who made any move to screw up the expedition, when you think back on it. If things had gone the way Wallace planned, they'd have arrested the rest of us, or worse, when we came busting out of the gumbo limbo. When Marlowe gunned Wallace while Gaston and I were wiping out his German pals, the other two had to lie low till they saw a chance to make a run for the base. Tonight they did. Next question."

Sylvia said, "I have one, Dick. You've about convinced me there was more to this treasure hunt than I could possibly have guessed. But what's the bloody point of it all? What on earth are Germans doing in Central America and why did Wallace go to so much trouble to do what?"

Captain Gringo took out a claro and lit it before he said, "Starting at the beginning: Once upon a time there was a Monroe Doctrine. It didn't and doesn't apply to the colonies that Great Britain, France, Spain, Holland, Denmark, and so forth already established over here before old Monroe got elected and protective. But Germany never managed to colonize much of anything, before Bismarck, and Bismarck comes after Monroe. So Germany can't openly build any bases on this side of the pond. But they say Kaiser Willy cheats at cards, too. A while back, Gaston and I were hired to find and mess up a German navy base on the Pacific coast. The one at Laguna Caratasca must be one that British Intelligence hasn't spotted yet. I thought at first they had, and that this was one of our old pal, Greystoke's, wild and wooly missions. But not even British Intelligence would be wild enough to saddle a mission with four women and a mess of rank greenhorns, no offense, so there's only one other way to read it. Wallace was making a *delivery*. He couldn't just sail in by sea. The Royal and U.S. navies patrol the Mosquito Coast regularly, in addition to the Honduran gunboats that one could bump noses with off the entrance of a supposedly deserted lagoon. Nobody would stop a yacht or schooner with proper papers and the Union Jack flapping long enough to matter. But there would be a record in the log of some allied vessel, and when and if that Panama Canal gets finished and somebody puts a torpedo into anybody anywhere near it, old records will get dug out a lot."

Bertie said, "Anyone can see the advantages to Germany of a secret navy base near the narrow waistline of the Americas, Dick. But you say Wallace was delivering something?"

"Yeah. Don't ask me what. Probably some new technical equipment. If it was simply information, a schooner passing by one night could just send it by wireless, since the Germans on shore have Marconi stuff handy. This arms race they're having since Kaiser Willy started scaring grown-ups with his temper tantrums has the invention business busy as hell. The diesel engine's only a couple of years old and the square heads are already stuffing 'em in their torpedo boats and experimental submersibles. Whatever Wallace was bringing them to modernize that base some more had to be small enough to hide in a steam car, but too heavy to carry on foot. That was the whole point of this otherwise crazy steam car jungle expedition. Wallace was too slick to have it in his own car. If it had been in the White I left Marlowe in, Marlowe could have swiped or sabotaged it. Ergo, it was in Gordon's steamer, and, since Gordon doesn't live here anymore, we'll probably never know what it was."

Bertie gasped. "My God! By now they've *delivered* it! No wonder they didn't need to steal extra fuel! The buggers drove straight for the lagoon to the east! But what will happen to Matilda, if she wasn't in on it?"

Captain Gringo shrugged and said, "Her husband will probably wind up with a flora-dora girl from the Windmill Theater. Some of her other friends might miss her."

Pat said, "Surely those Germans wouldn't do poor Matilda in, would they?"

He didn't answer. It was a stupid question, even coming from Pat, and there were more important matters to settle. He said, "Okay, let's forget about the German base and our former playmates. Now that we know it's there, if any of you feel patriotic you can write a letter to the *Times* or even ring up Whitehall when you get back to England. That's the problem we have to worry about. We're not going to be able to stay here long. By now the Germans know that we may be onto them, so they're not going to want any of us to get away, and, thanks to Gordon and Fenton, they'll find out where we are any minute!"

Gaston said, "I think we have a night's grace on them, Dick. Their two agents left before we returned with the news of that patrol we just wiped out. Even if they send out another, they won't find the bodies before dawn, *hein?*"

"Maybe. The patrol leader had a radio receiver. If they order him back and he doesn't come back, they could put two and two together without finding body one. Gordon and Fenton will tell them how good I am with that machine gun, if they haven't gotten the message by now. How far are we from the lagoon's big guns?"

Gaston was an old artillery officer, so he gulped and said, "*Merde*, not far enough!"

Bertie didn't seem to know much about long-range shell-fire. He asked, "Why did Wallace hire you two experts and issue you machine guns if the whole expedition was a ruse to deliver some thingamajig to his German friends, Dick?"

Captain Gringo shrugged and said, "Artistic touch, most likely. He had Marlowe down as a bum. Probably thought *our* reputation was overblown, too. Someone was sure to wonder why he'd take a mess of greenhorns out in the jungle with no security men at all. One of the guns was packed so it would have rusted to junk before we ever opened it. The other was screwed up more cleverly. The head spacing was set wrong and a couple of screws were loose when I field stripped it, cleaned it, and put it back together. He must have assumed I was a slam-bang hired tough who didn't do things like that. Besides, he was leading us into an ambush where it wouldn't have mattered if the Maxim worked or not. I screwed him up by taking my job more seriously than he'd expected. Let's not pick at scabs, Bertie. What's done is done. We have to get out of here pronto. You kiddies start loading the steam cars while I have a chat with the Indians. I take it nobody's still being silly about wanting to look for buried treasure?"

Not even Pat was that dumb, even if it meant having to explain to her rich relatives. Captain Gringo got up and went looking for Decepcióna. He couldn't ask any of the Indians where she was. So she found him by coming out of a hut to see why the kids and squaws were pointing at him and laughing so much. Decepcióna said, "You should not be at this end of the village without an interpreter. But I am at your service. The chief, my uncle, says I am to serve you in any way you wish."

He wasn't sure she meant that the way it sounded, even if she was standing there stark naked with mighty friendly eyes. He said, "Decepcióna, I've got some really tough translating for you indeed. Do you know what cannon are?"

"Of course. I am not an ignorant person."

"Good. You and your people have to move, pronto. The bad *blancos* have big cannon that can lob a shell many kilometers. Some other evil people may have told them we are here. If they did, I'm sorry, but this village is in danger of being blown to straw and splinters, *poco tiempo!*"

"We must tell the chief and elders. Come."

She took his hand and led him to a slightly larger hut. He still had to duck his head to enter, though the short Indian girl found the doorway high enough.

The young chief and old medicine man were seated around a little fire with some other important Mosquitoes. Decepcióna didn't seem to be mincing words as she opened up on them with machine-gun grunts and groans. Apparently she was a bright little gal who didn't have to chew the rag much when you told her about white men with big guns. The old *brujo* closed his eyes and began to recite a poem or something, but Decepcióna stamped her tiny bare foot and even Captain Gringo got her message when she flapped her hands and yelled, "Boom! Boom! Kawa-poof!"

The young chief was a natural survivor too. That probably was why they followed him. He shut the old man up and started giving orders in a no-bullshit tone as Decepcióna turned to Captain Gringo and said, "My uncle and great warrior says we can move at once to another camp where we used to live until the spirits of the soil refused us good crops. By now the thatch will have rotted away, but the campsite is already cleared and we know where the nearest water is. Do you think we will be safe there?"

"How far is it, Decepcióna?"

"Far. It will take us most of the night to walk there. Your big-wheeled things can roll faster than we can walk, but if you wish to come with us you must follow slowly."

Captain Gringo blinked in surprise and asked, "Are your

people still willing to accept us? I was afraid they'd be sore about us bringing all this trouble on them, Decepcióna!"

"Why should they be cross with you? You are our guests. The other ones are the evil persons who wish to make boom-boom, no?"

He smiled down at her gently and said, "I guess some people would look at it that way. A lot wouldn't. I think we should be safe a night's march away. There's no way even a hot-shot German gunnery officer could range on a target he has no way of picking out. Tell your chief I thank him, Decepcióna."

The pretty little naked girl shrugged and replied, "Why do you owe thanks to anyone? You have warned us. We shall heed your warning. We have treated you as friends. Now you have treated us as friends. Friends do not thank one another for doing what is only right. They help each other when they have a common enemy. Your people and my people are in this fight together, no?"


So the problem of whether he slept discreetly with Phoebe or had another shot at Sylvia just never came up that night. Instead of sleeping with anybody, they all got to tool along in the steam cars behind the marching Indians.

The Indians carried torches, so Sylvia in the lead with the Stanley didn't need her headlights to avoid things an Indian could step over but a Stanley had to steer around. The runty but strong Mosquitoes made good time afoot, although it was maddening slow driving. Not having the advantages of civilization, the Indians only had to carry small packs, consisting mostly of their few belongings wrapped in the hammocks each tribal member slept in. The young chief had seemed surprised and delighted when the whites offered to carry some of the heavy stuff in the steam cars.

Captain Gringo, Gaston, and the two girls got to talk more than they really needed to as they passed the night at less than five miles an hour. It was generally agreed that their best bet would be to hole up at the new Indian village long enough to let the Germans get tired of looking for them, then pile everyone and all the reserve kerosene in one steam car and make a beeline for Patuca, the first seaport up the coast. When Sylvia worried aloud about German agents intercepting them there before they could board a ship out, he explained, "They won't. They know that if we make it to any civilization and a telegraph office, their game is up. They never tried to rebuild that other secret base Gaston and I found for British Intelligence one time. The idea of a secret base is that it's a *secret*, see?"

Pat said, "Oh, I see, Dick. If we make it alive to Patuca, those horrid Germans will have to assume we've tattled on them whether we have or not. What will the Royal Navy do when we tell them about it, stand offshore and blow them to bits?"

"Hardly. That would call for a declaration of war, and I don't think either side will be ready to play out their family quarrel for at least twenty years. Queen Victoria will probably drop a note to her grandson, Kaiser Willy, chiding him for being so naughty. He'll probably tell her she has him all wrong and order his navy to build some other secret base within cruising range of Panama. There are oodles of places to choose from on both coasts of Central America."

Sylvia sighed and said, "It's all so infantile. This endless bickering between the great powers would read like a comic opera if only people didn't have to get killed over it all."

"Pawns are throwaway pieces in any chess game, doll. If the old Widow of Windsor and her half-crippled grandson thought they personally would have to lead the first pawns into battle, we could forget about the big war brewing over on your side of the pond. But the chess masters don't get put in the box, even when they lose the game, so we pawns have to look out for ourselves!"

Sylvia shuddered and said, "I always thought Matilda was a natural survivor. Why do you suppose she did such a stupid thing, Dick?"

He knew, but it wouldn't have been gallant, or sensible, to say so. So he said, "She probably thought she was surviving pretty good. When she caught those guys loading up, they'd naturally have told her they were just punking out and driving back to Nicaragua because the fun and games were getting rough."

Pat said, "I'm glad she left with them. She was terribly stuck up. At least now we know we can all trust one another, right, Dick?"

It was a good question. Gaston, too, had obviously been thinking about it. He said, *"Eh bien.* We agree British Intelligence can't know about the place or it would not be there, whatever the late Marlowe was about to find out if he was working for anyone. Any other confederates of Wallace would have left with Gordon and Fenton. Ergo, all that is left are eight great fools, since I must in all justice include myself among the used and *très* abused. Eight people can ride in one steam car, if pretty girls do not mind sitting in the laps of gallant gentlemen. Who get's Phoebe, Dick?"

"That's up to her," said Captain Gringo, kicking him to shut him up. The damned old lecher obviously thought he'd found Sylvia sleeping off a swell time with him. This was hardly the time and place to explain.

Long before sunrise they had run out of things to say, so they hadn't said much for hours when the light started getting better. A little while later they rolled out into a clearing, or what would have been a clearing if the weeds hadn't already grown shoulder high. The Indians went right to work with their machetes as the three remaining steam cars parked in line under the trees and everyone got out wearily to watch the Indians make camp.

Rome wasn't built in a day, but the Mosquitoes weren't Romans, so they didn't mess around. For people supposed to be lazy ignorant savages, they were organized better than some military outfits Captain Gringo could remember. New huts sprouted like mushrooms as the womenfolk got fires going and put on the pots to boil mush. Before Captain Gringo could suggest it, the young chief sent his scouts out to secure the perimeter and, hopefully, bag some game for said pots.

Decepcióna came over to the whites to tell them their new quarters were ready. Sylvia sniffed thoughtfully as the naked Indian girl took Captain Gringo's hand and led him the length of the village. She took him to a small but well-thatched hut with one big hammock slung between its two main poles. She turned to face him in the shade of the windowless hut. Her proud firm breasts still looked great in the dim light as she said, calmly, "The chief says you must all be tired and there is nothing for you to do here anyway. Would you like to sleep now, Dick? Or do you wish to make love to me first?"

He laughed and asked, "Do I have a choice?"

"Of course. You are a guest. Everything we have to offer is yours. I have nothing to offer but myself. If you do not think I am pretty, I can find another girl for you. But none of them speak Spanish."

"That's very generous indeed. Do you want to sleep with me, Decepcióna?"

She lowered her lashes modestly and said, "I don't know. I have never made love to any white man, let alone a giant. I think I am afraid, a little. But if you want me, I have no choice. The chief says we are to make you feel at home while you are with us."

He said, "I think you are very pretty. I think you're scared to death, too. Why don't we just be friends awhile until we've both had time to get used to the idea?"

She smiled up at him radiantly and said, "Oh, you are so understanding. I think you are pretty, too. But a woman needs a little time to make up her mind. I was so afraid you would treat me roughly. I had decided to be brave, but . . ."

"I understand, honey. Why don't you go out and play with the other children?"

She didn't seem to like that much. But she ducked out, muttering something about seeing who was a child, maybe later.

He hung up his things and consulted his watch. He'd just spent a long full night and they faced a long dull day. He'd nibbled field rations in the Stanley driving from the other camp, so who wanted Indian mush or any breakfast at all? That hammock looked inviting and he didn't know when he'd have to do some serious traveling without sleep again, so he peeled off his duds and climbed in naked. The Indians hadn't provided a top sheet. People who wandered naked in broad daylight had small need of modesty in bed, and he knew that most Indians wouldn't dream of entering a sleeping hut without singing about it outside a lot, waiting for an invitation to enter.

He stretched lazily and settled into the womblike cotton webbing to close his eyes and, he hoped, catch up on his sleep. He'd almost made it when Sylvia's voice said, "Oh, here you are. Alone, I see. What's the matter, didn't you like that little squaw?"

He opened one eye and growled, "Decepcióna is a lady, which is more than I can say for some dames I know. What the hell do you want now, another game of prick-tease? It's only fair to warn you I'm not wearing my pants today. If you want to sleep with me again, all previous contracts are null and void."

"Do you have to speak to me in that tone, Dick?"

"I didn't want to speak to you at all. This is the second time you've come in to pester me while I was trying to get some shut-eye. What the hell's wrong with you, Sylvia? Can't you find someone else to tease?"

"I don't understand you, Dick. Why do you keep calling me a tease?"

He sat up, his nudity still partially hidden by the sagging webbing, and growled, "Oh, for God's sake, let's get it over with!" as he reached out an arm, grabbed her around her slim waist, and hauled her in.

The unexpected move threw her off kilter, or she wanted him to think it had. At any rate, he pulled her half-atop him, put his other arm around her neck, and kissed her good. Her mouth had popped open in a surprised gasp as their lips met, so he tongued her deeply while he was at it. She couldn't say anything but put up a struggle, a mild one at any rate, as he hauled her half-aboard the hammock.

Fighting for balance, if that was what she was doing, Sylvia spread her legs wide as she was bent over him. He shifted his weight, sliding both their heads and shoulders up higher on the half-moon of the hammock. Then he groped with his left hand down across his own lap, grabbing Sylvia behind her right thigh, and lifted her right foot from the ground as she protested mutely with his lips on hers and struggled for balance with the one foot she was left standing on.

He pulled her right knee across the hammock and hooked it over the far side with her high button shoe flailing wildly a long way from the dirt floor. Naturally her skirt had been forced up above her hips by the forced split across the hammock. She caught on to his full intent and whimpered as well as she was able, while sucking his tongue. But he ignored her protest, if it was a protest, and since his shaft was already at full attention by now, all he had to do was thrust up with his hips once he'd pulled the elastic leg opening of her loose silk pantaloons aside, and . . .

"No!" She gasped, twisting her lips from his as he entered her. But he soothed, "Yes indeed!" as he put both hands around to cup her buttocks in his palms and pull her on like a glove. A nice tight glove filled with whipped cream.

She sobbed that he was a brute even as she hopped on her left foot to get into a more comfortable position with one knee hooked over each side rope of the hammock and spitted herself on him to the roots. He started bouncing his hips and the hammock bounced too as she fell weakly against his chest, sobbing, "You're *touching* me, damn you!"

"I noticed. It'd feel even better if we got you out of all those damned clothes."

He stopped, but noticed she was still bouncing the hammock as she protested, "That's not what I came in here for, you bastard. I only wanted to ask you . . . Oh, my God, I'm coming!"

That made two of them. As he held her close, kissing her as he ejaculated in her widespread groin, he was too polite to say that he knew damn well she'd come in here to come. Why the hell did a widow who knew how to move so swell with a man inside her have to carry on like a virgin?

Apparently Sylvia had come to the same conclusion, now that she'd come. When they came up for air, she said, "It feels so silly doing it with my knickers on."

"Let's get you out of all that stuff, then."

"Oh, Dick, I couldn't. It's broad daylight. What if someone comes?"

"You'd look just as silly with your clothes on, and who needs to come in here but *us?* Be reasonable, honey, we've sparred around long enough."

She sighed and sat up to start undressing, with his help, with her thighs still spread and him still in her. As they got her skirt and blouse off over her head, he saw he'd been wrong about her wearing a corset. The tiny waist above the hem of her pantaloons measured less than twenty inches, which was surprising when you considered her chest measurement had to be close to forty. She leaned her big firm breasts against his chest as she asked, "How are we to get my knickers off without taking it out? I don't want to let you go soft at a time like this! I suppose you know I've been gushing for you since first we met?"

"The feeling was mutual. Ain't it a bitch how much time grown people waste being shy? Get off on my left, between the hammock and the wall. I promise I won't let you down."

He didn't. As Sylvia finished peeling, with her back to the thatch, she saw his erection for the first time and gasped, "Oh, my God, was all that just in me? No wonder I came so unexpectedly!"

"Hey, Sylvia, we agreed to cut the maidenly bullshit, okay? Hold it. I'll get out and let you be on the bottom this time."

As he stood up to join her, Sylvia looked dubiously at the deep cup of the empty hammock and asked, "Would it work that way?"

He followed her meaning. He took her in his arms again, held her now nude curves against his own naked flesh, and said, "You're probably right. I'd break my spine trying to go old-fashioned in a saggy hammock. But where there's a will there's a way."

He reached down and fumbled it into place as he bent his knees. Sylvia stood on tiptoe to help, but asked, "Can anyone really do it standing up? Oh, I see they can!"

It worked even better when she raised her legs to wrap them around his waist as he held her by the big soft buttocks that matched her hourglass upper story so well. But it was tiring as well as inspiring and they wound up on the dirt floor, pounding hard, and she didn't object until she'd come again. Then, she naturally made a dumb remark about feeling beastly to be rutting in the dirt like an animal.

He rolled her on her hands and knees politely to brush the red grains of jungle laterite from her naked back and fanny as he finished dog-style. She protested that this was most undignified, too, but she didn't ask him to stop, and arched her spine for it all when he came in her again.

As she crouched there like a ruddy piggy, as she put it, she pulsed warmly on his shaft as she murmured, "Well, I signed up for adventure, and I must say this is perishing *unusual!* Do you have any other obscene lovemaking left for me to endure, you brute?"

He said, "Sure. Let me show you how you really do it in a hammock."

He helped her to her feet, sat her crossways in the hammock with the nearest rope under her tail bone and the other supporting the nape of her neck. She said, "This is silly. Where do you fit in, darling?"

He spread her pale thighs wide, then stepped closer, and, still standing on his bare feet, put it in her again, saying, "We call this playing swing."

"Good God, you're still hard and . . . What are you *doing?*"

It was a dumb question. As he started to swing her a few inches each way, not moving his own hips but sliding her the full length of his inspiration each way, she closed her eyes, bit her lips, and forgot about asking dumb questions as he sort of jerked himself off with her, further inspired by the full view of her beautiful face and nude hourglass torso bobbing faster than he'd have ever managed to move his own hips.

She spread her thighs wider, cupped a breast in each hand, and moaned, "Oh, God, I just died and went to heaven!" And he could tell by her internal contractions that she was climaxing yet again. He closed his eyes and grabbed for the hammock rope on either side of her head to lay half-atop her as he came in her again, kissing her as her long black hair came unpinned and fell down almost to sweep the dirt floor.

He'd just satisfied them both for the moment and was coming up for air when another female voice gasped, "Oh!" and he looked up, feeling like a shit-eating dog, to see Phoebe standing in the doorway.

Before he could say anything, his other girl had turned and

flounced out of sight. Sylvia murmured dreamily, "Did you say something, darling?"

"No, Phoebe just walked in on us. She must shock easy. She's gone."

Sylvia stiffened and gasped, "Oh, my God! How will I ever explain to her? The poor little spinster knows nothing about a real woman's needs!"

He said, "Uh, I'd better explain to her. Hold the fort. I'll be right back."

"You can't talk to that poor little sparrow after she's just seen you rutting like a stallion with me! My God, I don't know how I'll ever face her again myself!"

He slowly withdrew from her as he soothed, "You're not thinking, doll box. She saw me. She didn't see you. You were on the bottom, so all she could see was the top of your head. We were smart enough to pile your things behind this hammock, see?"

"Don't be an ass! Who else is she going to think it could have been? It certainly wasn't she, and Pat had flaming red hair! I'm the only dark brunette left."

"No, you're not. We're in an Indian village. Hear me, pretty squaw, I go now to make peace with white lady peeping Tom. You stay here. Keep-um wig-wam warm."

As she got it, Sylvia laughed hysterically and said, "By George, it just might work! I'm not about to stay *here,* though! Let me up so I can dress and think up a very ingenious excuse for not being otherwise in sight when that silly little thing popped in at us!"

He didn't argue. He wanted to head Phoebe off at the pass before she said something dumb to one of the others. He quickly dressed and went out looking for her. He found her talking to Bertie. He moved closer, nodded pleasantly to Bertie, and said, "Would you excuse us a moment, Bertie? I think Phoebe wants to cuss me out in private."

Phoebe stamped her foot, stared angrily at him through her

slightly fogged glasses, and said, "We've nothing more to say to each other, ever again, you perishing squaw man!"

Bertie, ever the peace maker, said, "Come now, Phoebe, boys will be boys and all that. Our captain's no doubt been cultivating the natives, eh what?"

"I saw what he was doing to that damned Indian bitch. Which hut are you in, Bertie?"

"Uh, that one over there. Why?"

"Never mind. I want a word with you in private. Do you follow me, Dick?"

"I'm not about to follow you kiddies. Never let it be said I'm not a good loser. Sorry, Phoebe. Lost my head."

"I've noticed you do that a lot, you bastard!" Phoebe snapped, taking the bewildered Bertie by the arm to lead him away to his doom.

Captain Gringo grinned as he watched them duck inside Bertie's hut. Bertie had said he kind of liked her, so all was well that ended well, and, while old Phoebe was a great little lay, so was Sylvia, and Sylvia was the best-looking thing in miles, hot damn!

He ran into Sylvia near the hut the Indians had built for her. They'd been very generous in giving all eight members of the party individual quarters, but he supposed the saplings and thatch didn't cost much. As he joined Sylvia he murmured, "She bought it. Let's go back and see if we left anything out."

"God, no! With my luck, the next time she popped in I'd be on top!"

"She won't. I think she just shacked up with Bertie for the day."

"Phoebe? Shacked up? That's silly, darling. I doubt that poor old dried-up Phoebe's ever even kissed a man in her life!"

He had no way of telling her how wrong she was without having two girls mad at him. So he just shrugged and said, "Well, they're sure up to something in Bertie's hut. Let's go back to mine."

"Not until after dark at least, dear. They're probably just gossiping and I don't want to take that chance with my reputation. We both live in the same West End, after all. Haven't I satisfied you enough to last you until dark at least?"

He laughed, said he'd see her around the campus, and moved on to his own hut as she ducked into hers. He didn't see Pat or Gaston anywhere. That seemed logical. Wilson and Jerome had either found squaws, each other, or just wanted to be out of the sun. It was getting pretty high.

Decepcióna was reclining in his hammock when he ducked under the low entrance. He laughed and said, *"Now* I have an Indian to show Phoebe. I don't imagine she'll be back, though. What can I do for you, Decepcióna?"

"I am here to do for you. Now that I see you are gentle, I am no longer afraid of your great size and funny-colored hair. Do you have yellow hair all over, Dick person?"

"Uh, I'd love to show you, and I hope I'm still man enough. But is there any way to lock these doors, *querida mia?* It feels silly to have people popping in unexpectedly."

The Indian girl rolled out of the hammock, and as she took his hand he stared down at her compact brown nudity and decided he wasn't as worn out as he'd thought. She said, "We can go for a walk in the trees if you like. Our chief has ordered that none of our people are to go near your horseless carriages. But you can go. And I can go as your guest, no? If you would rather make love in the fallen leaves, I am willing, but it is not comfortable and people make jokes when a girl comes back with black stains on her behind."

He said the parked cars sounded like a neat idea. So they went out to them and it was. They climbed into the backseat of Bertie's steamer, since it was parked between the others and offered more privacy. The little Indian girl marveled at the luxurious feel of the padded leather seats as she rubbed her bare bottom on the backseat, experimentally, and lay back to spread her brown thighs and say, "I think I want you very much. You are very pretty."

He said she was pretty, too, as he quickly undressed, hung his duds over the back of the passenger seat, and got to his knees on the floorboards between Decepcióna's welcomingly spread knees. She moved her childish-looking hairless groin to meet him as she said, "Oh, you *are* yellow-haired all over, but I'm not sure we will fit."

They did. She stared at him wide-eyed in wonder as he slid into what only looked inexperienced on the outside. Inside, Decepcióna was all woman, and he didn't have to feel shitty about taking advantage of a trusting child of nature.

Like most sensible so-called primitives, the Mosquitoes saw no point in depriving themselves of one of the few real pleasures life offered people who didn't collect stamps or grow orchids in a green house. As she started moving skillfully, complimenting him on having the biggest dong she'd ever had in her up to now, it was obvious why the naked Indians felt no shame wandering around like that. By the time they grew up they'd probably laid everyone of the opposite sex in the tribe. So it was no more embarrassing to walk around in front of old lovers than it would be for a married white couple to see each other naked in private, although some white women he'd met complained that their husbands had been a little silly about night shirts, come to think of it.

He wondered why he was thinking at all as the sprightly little squaw slid her tight box skillfully up and down his shaft, doing most of the work. She was breathing faster but was still under control as she said, conversationally, "You do it well, *querido.* I enjoy it when a man takes his time in me. Is it all right if I let myself go now? Forgive me, I am trying to make it last for you, but your unusual penis makes me most hot and I am excited as a girl doing it for the first time!"

He realized he'd been neglecting her, so he started pounding as he bent over to take her upper body in his arms and kissed her as she came in a series of hard bumps and grinds that inspired him to return the compliment. As they lay limply together, Decepcióna opened her eyes to croon dreamily, "Oh, that is what you people call kissing, no? It felt very strange. Even a little dirty. But would you do it again?"

He did, letting her start the action again because in truth he was a little soft from overwork. But he didn't stay that way for long. For a girl who didn't know much about kissing, she sure was learning to tongue nicely, suddenly, and you didn't have to work to keep it up in Decepcióna. You just had to hang on and let her screw like a mink.

She came even faster the second time. He faked an orgasm to be polite. It still felt great in there, but, like these steam cars, he had only so much reserve fuel, and Sylvia had been great too.

By the time Decepcióna went limp in postclimactic contentment, he was inspired enough again at least to keep moving gently. She purred, "Oh, you wish more? I am so happy you liked me so much. I like you very much, too. But could we not rest a few moments, *querido?* We have all day, you know."

She gave him one last promising grind as she added coyly, "The night, too. I can't wait until you swing me in your hammock."

He laughed and sat up to hold her head against his shoulder. He hadn't thought he'd invented that hammock position. But he hadn't considered the coming night. Sylvia had promised to come back to his hammock too, and if she caught him playing swing with a real Indian squaw, oh boy!

He was about to ask Decepcióna how seriously she took going steady when all hell started breaking loose. The little squaw stiffened in his arms and gasped in fear as a heavy shell whistled down to explode in the not-too-distant distance!

He rolled out of the steamer with Decepcióna under one arm like a football as he ran for the nearest big tree, swung around to the far side, and flopped down atop her to shield her with his body as another shell shook the earth under them. The girl gasped, "What is happening? It sounds like the end of the world!"

It did. The once-solid earth heaved in rippling shock waves under them as he lay naked atop her. Somehow, as the barrage went on a year or more, his penis found its way back inside her trembling vagina between her open trembling thighs. Neither of them noticed. They were too worried about staying alive to notice that they were screwing. He counted at least fifty shell bursts, big eight-inchers, from the sound of them. Then it got very quiet, save for the distant keening of a wailing woman.

Decepcióna said, "Let me up! I have to go see what happened to my village!"

But he said, "Stay put. I know what happened to your village. The motherfuckers may play the old second-salvo trick."

"Second what?"

"They stop the barrage to let the survivors get up and wander around looking for dead and wounded. Then, with everyone on their feet, another salvo slams down and . . . hey, have you noticed we seem to be making love again?"

"Yes, it feels very nice, even on the ground. But I am worried about my people."

"I am too. We can't help 'em if we get killed, and we've got good cover here. Hm, could you raise your knees a little?"

She did, locking her ankles around his waist as she took him deeper. That seemed to make her lose interest in getting up for a while, so they were going at it hot and heavy when the second barrage started. It lasted even longer. At least a hundred eight-inchers screamed down through the forest canopy to deafen their ears and quiver the ground like jelly under them as they went on making love. It was no dumber a thing to be doing at a time like this than anything else they could think of, and he was as willing to die coming in the arms of a beautiful girl as he was anywhere else.

When the shelling stopped, Decepcióna giggled and said, "I don't know if it was the fear or the fucking, but I have never come that well before!"

He said, "Yeah, but we'd better get some clothes on. *I* have to, I mean. It should be safe to take a peek now."

He led her back to the steamer and put her back in the seat as he dressed quickly, saying, "You stay here. If I'm wrong and they lob a third salvo, I may never speak to you again."

"I want to come too."

"You just did. Stay here, damm it. Like your chief must say, I have spoken!"

He left her there and legged it into the village, or, rather, what was left of it. The clearing was mostly holes in the ground, but the frames of a few huts were still standing, their thatch blown away. He gagged as he saw half an Indian baby sprawled on the lip of a crater. A mangled squaw lay beyond. He responded to a low groan to find the old *brujo* sitting in the bottom of yet another shell crater, trying to hold his guts in with both hands. He wasn't able to. As the old man looked up at him in mute agony, Captain Gringo knelt at his side, smiled, and pulled out his gun with a silent question in his eyes. The old man stared soberly at the .38 and nodded. So Captain Gringo put the muzzle against his temple and pulled the trigger to put him out of his misery.

The sound of the shot brought a shout he recognized as Gaston's, thank God. As he climbed out of the shell crater, Gaston came over the broken ground to him, muttering, "*Sacre*, I told you they were Boche! Who but a child-molesting licker of pig shit would shell an innocent native village without even a declaration of annoyance, let alone war?"

"When you're right, you're right. What happened to our people?"

"Phoebe and Jerome did not make it. When the first shell hit, Pat was most fortunately on top, so I just picked her up and ran through the side of the hut with her. I just found her clothes, and she'll join us when she puts them on in the bushes."

"Great minds think alike. What about Bertie, Wilson, and Sylvia?"

"Out in the trees to the northwest, I told them to stay there while I came back to look for your body. By the way, why didn't I *find* your body, Dick? You certainly were not here when that second salvo landed!"

"Long story. How did our Indian friends make out?"

"Not well, I fear. Like the rest of us, most made it out from under the first short salvo. Everyone tends to run like the hell at such times. But then, though I tried to warn them, the poor fools came back into the target area in response to the cries of the wounded. I shouted myself to a face of blue, but naturally none of them understood me. The chief is over that way, what is left of him. I think the triple-titted Boche killed over half the band. If they got that girl who speaks Spanish, we may be in trouble."

"They didn't. Decepcióna made it out with me. She's over by the cars. I think we'd better get everybody, red *and* white, over by the cars. We've got to get the hell *out* of here, *poco tiempo!*"

"*Oui.* I too was astounded to be shelled in such a tranquil Garden of Eden! How on earth could the murderous eaters of pig shit have ranged on us so tightly, Dick? That was no harassing fire. Every one of those shells was aimed. Most landed at the end of the village where we were staying! I do not believe it could have been luck, but how could they have pinpointed us after we drove through the jungle all night?"

"Easy. Tell you about it after we get everyone together by the cars."

• • •

Captain Gringo went back to where he'd left Decepcióna in the backseat of Bertie's steam car while Gaston went to round up the survivors. The Indian girl said she was ready to make love again. But he told her to put her mental pantaloons back on and explained what he wanted her to tell the Indians as she gathered them together and brought them out there in the trees.

He had a few moments alone as he looked the cars over, trying to decide which was the best to keep. Overloaded, they'd need the most powerful engine and the best set of tires to make it out of this mess. Wheels, like kerosene tins, could easily be switched around. A lot of camping gear would have to be left behind and it would still be a tight fit.

Gaston hailed him. He looked over to see the little Frenchman leading Bertie, Wilson, and the two surviving girls toward the last three cars. The whites seemed subdued and shaken by recent happenings. Save for Pat, who'd been carried, they'd all made it the same way, simply by crashing through the nearest thatch wall and running like hell when the first big shell had slammed down. Wilson grumbled that he'd been beating Jerome at rummy at the time and that Jerome still owed him. Sylvia and Pat were too ashen-faced to say anything.

Bertie asked if the cars had been damaged. Captain Gringo shook his head and said, "No, of course not. They were parked well clear of the target area, you son of a bitch!"

Bertie blinked in astonishment, then replied, "I say, there's no need to be nasty, captain! I feel terrible about what happened to poor Phoebe, too!"

Captain Gringo said, "I'll bet you do. She was a good kid, you two-faced prick!"

Then, since Bertie was going for his gun, Captain Gringo beat him to the draw and blew his face off! He was so pissed that he emptied the rest of the chambers into Bertie's twitching corpse as it sprawled in the muck at his feet.

Gaston whipped out his own gun and snapped, "The rest of you should stand ever so still, *hein? I* don't know why he did that, either, but I'm still on his side!"

Wilson stared wide-eyed at Bertie's dead body and gasped. "Have you gone mad, Walker?" he asked.

Captain Gringo shook his head as he calmly proceeded to reload his smoking .38. He said, "The prick was working for the other side. We have him to thank for that double salvo just now. He left Phoebe to die messy, too, unless he killed her instead of just knocking her out before he got an early lead on the rest of you. He knew when and where the shells would land, so naturally he was out in the trees long before the first one came in. He'd have had a time explaining that to Phoebe. She was on *our* side!"

Sylvia licked her lips and asked, "Dick, how could you possibly know all this?"

Captain Gringo holstered his gun and said, "Process of elimination. You can put your gun away now, Gaston. There's nobody here but us dupes, now."

Gaston lowered his revolver politely, but kept it in his hand as he growled, *"Sacre* God damn, I wish you'd explain, Dick."

Wilson nodded and added, "Bloody right! I've known Bertie for years. He was British to the bone, or at least he was until just now!"

Captain Gringo sighed and said, "Jesus, do I have to do all the thinking around here? Yeah, I guess I do. Wallace didn't pick any of you for your knowlege of power politics. Okay, as you all know, once upon a time the German high command wanted to deliver something to a secret base. It was probably something like a new wireless set. Since Marconi patented his wireless telegraph a couple of years ago, hardly a month goes by without someone coming up with another patented improvement, and the Germans lead in the new technology. They got a head start because radio waves were discovered by a German named Hertz back in '87."

He reached for a smoke and lit up before he continued, "Okay, Der Kaiser likes to keep his navy up to date, secret or not. It wouldn't stay secret with the Royal Navy patrolling the Caribbean if they sent new radio tubes by parcel post or tried to smuggle them in by sea. So first they hired a cashiered British officer named Wallace. It takes money to belong to the best London clubs. Wallace and his confederates recruited the bunch of you with his mammy-jamming treasure-hunt story, knowing that anyone from Whitehall who got wind of the expedition would dismiss it as a pathetic waste of time and money by a bunch of well-to-do eccentrics. Then things started to go wrong. Marlowe, hired both as a guide and as more cover, caught on, somehow, before we'd even left Puerto Cabezas. He may have been a worthless remittance man, but, unlike Wallace, he was a patriot who read the papers and wasn't happy about Kaiser Willy's obvious future plans. After Gaston and I messed up the welcoming committee, Marlowe beat Wallace to the draw, and Wallace was an old soldier who should have been good. Bertie was even better. He drew on Marlowe and killed him with Marlowe *already* having the drop on him! It takes a real gun slick to do that, so Bertie was no mere West End playboy."

Gaston cut in, *"Merde alors,* this is all ancient history, Dick. One can see how you might have suspected there was more to Bertie than met the eye. But you just shot him *très* seriously, and if that was all you had to go by . . ."

"It wasn't," said Captain Gringo. "I didn't know for sure until today. Those shells just now didn't drop out of the sky by accident. They were lobbed at least twenty-five miles, with pinpoint accuracy!"

The redhead, Pat, asked. "Couldn't those other sneaks have told the nasty Germans where we were, Dick?"

He shook his head and asked, "How? The whole point of moving under cover of darkness was that Baxter and Fenton knew where we were when they left with Matilda. I knew before the last shells landed that we were under pinpoint fire. Like I said, the rest was elimination. I knew you girls were unable to send wireless messages from your car. Gaston and I were in it with you every time you were. Wilson had been riding with his fellow Scot, Gordon, and Jerome was sitting in the back of the White we abandoned in the river until we had to reshuffle some. Bertie had been driving the same steamer from start to finish. Look at those headlights, Gaston. It's time you won a gold star from the teacher."

Gaston stared morosely at the brass headlights of the late Bertie's steamer and said, *"Eh bien,* they are mundane electric lights. So what?"

"So what? Most steamers come with carbide lamps. There's no point in having an electric battery in a goddamn *steamer!* I just looked under the chassis. There's a magneto geared to the steam engine that turns the wheels. As it rolls it charges a lead-cell battery. A big one. Bigger than anyone would need to light those tiny Edison bulbs."

*"Sacre bleu!* Are you saying Bertie betrayed our position with a secret radio transmitter?"

"He didn't send smoke signals. The setup's pretty slick. The steel chassis itself is the antenna. The only indication of the transmitting tubes hidden by the dash is one little wire spliced to the ones from the battery to said headlights. It's part of the same circuit. So all he had to do to send dots and dashes with others sitting right next to him would be to fiddle with his headlight switch. Who pays attention?"

"But, Dick, my beloved electrician, would not we have noticed if he'd been blinking his headlights so madly?"

"Sure we would have, if they'd been blinking. How did you think I found the transmitter? I just tried to turn the headlights on as I was inspecting all three cars. His bulbs had been unscrewed and both sockets were empty when I looked closer through the thick dusty glass. I wondered why anyone would go to so much trouble to have electric headlights and then not have them. The rest is history."

Gaston nodded and said, *"Eh bien,* it does seem to add up. When the ones working with him deserted to make the delivery, he stayed behind to make certain none of us would ever wander out of the jungle all bedraggled to gossip about mysterious armed men we'd encountered in an area where poor Honduras doesn't even try to collect taxes, *non?"*

Captain Gringo didn't answer. Decepcióna was leading in a mess of leftover Indians. Most of them were women and children, thank God. The men had been the suckers who'd run back to help their injured and been hit by the second salvo. Those men left, about a dozen, seemed mad as hell about it. Some of them had smeared themselves with black grease and all of them were waving their longbows around in angry gestures.

Decepcióna said, "I told my people what you said about having to move again. They do not wish to move. They want to stand and fight. Those evil *blancos* killed our *brujo,* our chief, and many others. They say that if you will lead them, you can be our new chief. They know little about fighting men with such big guns!"

Captain Gringo smiled gently at her and said, "That seems obvious. Tell them I'm sure they are brave men and good archers, but that bows and arrows aren't much use against heavy weapons."

"Pooh, *you* also have a heavy weapon, Dick person! Your big gun that goes tom-tom-tom! Our bowmen know this country. They say they can scout and pick off the outposts of the bad *blancos.* You and your tom-tom-tom can deal with larger numbers, no?"

"Tell them we'll talk about it after we make camp somewhere else. This place is bad medicine. More shells could land any minute."

• • •

Captain Gringo and the other whites had plenty of time to think as they followed the Indians in Sylvia's and Bertie's steamers after abandoning the other, minus its tires. Sylvia's Stanley was a more powerful vehicle, but that half-assed attempt on his life had scorched her tires, and as long as they were low on kerosene anyway, it paid to make sure of good rubber. They had a lot of rolling to do. He'd been tempted to pile them all into Bertie's car alone, since he wanted to hang on to that wireless set. But the Indians said the hollow they knew of wasn't far, so why ride cramped before they had to? He and Gaston switched to the sneaky Bertie's vehicle to let Wilson and Jerome ride with the two girls for a change. The heavy gear they really might need rode in the empty seat behind him and Gaston. He naturally resisted any temptation to fiddle with switches as they drove.

It took their Indian comrades longer to set up camp again. They were sort of short-handed. Captain Gringo never would have chosen the site, had not those heavy shells made hash out of the last one. But Decepcióna and her tribesfolk caught on fast, for primitives. The new camp was set in a depression between two heavily wooded rises that were islands in the rainy season. The results were soggy dirt floors for the new huts erected with skilled machete carpentry. He saw why they slept in those hammocks and knew that the bugs would be a bitch after dark. But a mosquito bite didn't hurt half as much as an eight-inch shell coming through the thatch.

Some of the Indian women started building smudge fires, with the bugs in mind. He told Decepcióna to tell them not to send up any smoke before dark, and once again they surprised him by catching on quickly. His remaining white allies had been chosen for being slow learners. The Mosquito Indians were the product of selective evolution in an environment where the dull-of-wit didn't grow up to have children. As he sat on the running board of Bertie's steamer with Gaston, watching their smooth but quick movements, he said, "Dammit Gaston, I *like* these people!"

Gaston said, "I am not displeased with them, and I know what you are thinking, Dick. Forget it. Once the chase cools off, our only chance is a run for Patuca and a boat out. The Germans will be in enough trouble if our *white* friends make it out alive. Having found out about their thrice-accursed secret navy base, we owe it to Kaiser Willy to see that Whitehall hears all about it, *non?*"

"Yeah. I like that part. But it'll take weeks for the Royal Navy to make up its mind to do anything about it. Those square heads will want to tidy up before they leave. They know, now, that these Indians know too much, and the poor little bastards only have bows and arrows!"

"Poison arrows, Dick. Besides, those Boche can't catch many Indians in their own jungle, *hein?*"

"If they catch *one,* it'll be too many. Besides, these little guys are really pissed off. If we leave them on their own, some young braves are sure to try something to avenge all the relatives they just lost. The Germans will be expecting them to, too, dammit!"

Gaston said, *"C'est la* fucking *vie,* Dick. I agree they could use some strategic planning if they wish to make war on the German Reich. But I happen to be a military genius, so I know how hopeless attacking that base would be, even with our help."

"They probably have diesel fuel over there, you know."

"That is *très ridicule,* even coming from you! We have enough kerosene left for one car to steam as far as Patuca, or at least within walking distance of the port. The girls can sit on the laps of Wilson and Jerome in the back, with enough room left over for such few supplies as we need. If you insist on taking along the Maxim, I volunteer to hold her in *my* lap! It's over, Dick. We have managed to survive. When one considers how Wallace planned it all, I would say that all in all we have done better than expected. Now it is time to think of our remaining asses, *hein?*"

Decepcióna was coming over to them, smiling wearily and looking shiny as hell. She had smeared herself from head to toe with some sort of bug oil. It looked sort of sexy. Captain Gringo wondered what it would feel like to make love to such a slippery little brown body.

On the other hand, Sylvia might want to try covering her own naked hourglass with that stuff. If he could talk either girl into a slippery game of three in a hammock . . . Never mind, it would probably kill him.

Decepcióna told them their hammocks were ready when they were. She ran a small brown hand over her shiny naked tummy and added, "This place will be very bad after dark, Deek. The missionaries explained how you *blancos* feel about letting people see your bodies, but unless you can get your friends to follow sensible customs, the little flying fiends who dwell here will eat you all alive after dark."

Captain Gringo nodded. Then he frowned and said, "Wait a minute. How much of that goo have you people got on hand and what in hell is it?"

Decepcióna said, "It is just oil with juice the mosquitoes do not like mixed in with it, Dick person. We make it from the oil of nuts and the juice of a grass your people call citronella. The Spanish introduced the foreign grass long ago. It is one of the few favors they ever did us. We have many jars prepared. More than enough for everyone."

He grinned and said, "I thought I recognized the smell. We didn't smear it on quite as thick in the summer back in Connecticut. That's probably why it didn't work so hot. Could you spare us enough to fill at least two kerosene tins, Decepcióna?"

"Of course. Anything we have is yours, Dick person. But I must say your people must want to spread it very thickly on themselves if you need that much!

Gaston caught on. He nodded and said, *"Eh bien,* it ought to burn as well as kerosene, and the exhaust will do wonders for the insects, as we drive both cars, after all!"

Captain Gringo sent the Indian girl for the oil before he told Gaston, "Two cars makes the difference. We'll keep this one, with the radio gear. Sylvia can drive on to Patuca with Pat and the two useless men."

*"Merde alors,* Pat is not useless, Dick! She gives a *très fantastique* blow job!"

"I'll ask Decepcióna if she can find a friend for you. Most of them don't even know how to kiss, but they seem to be willing pupils. I'm sort of fond of Sylvia, too. It can't be helped. Someone has to get word to the outside world about that secret base. It may as well be four poor dupes who'd be of little use to us in a firefight."

Gaston gasped, *"Mon Dieu,* what is this nonsense about a firefight? If you are seeking volunteers to charge madly at people armed with eight-inch field guns, do not look at *me,* you maniac!"

Captain Gringo shrugged and said, "Okay, the others would probably be safer if you went along with them in Sylvia's steamer."

"That is the simple truth, for a change. But that leaves you, this steam car, a dozen naked savages, and a rusty machine gun low on ammunition to do . . . *what,* for God's sake?"

"Pay those Germans back, of course. I said I liked these Indians. Phoebe was a good kid, too."

Gaston sighed and said, "I never got any of that, but I'll take your word that she looked better without her glasses. You are still out of your mind, Dick. You only know the general direction of the base. You have no idea of the numbers, the weapons, or the dispositions of their defense perimeter!"

"That's where Indian scouts come in. I don't intend to drive in beeping Bertie's horn, for chrissake. Why don't you go tell the others? I hate long goodbyes, and there's no reason for any of you to hang around here getting bitten, once we get the extra oil."

Gaston said, "I hate long goodbyes too. I make it an overnight drive to Patuca, by compass. I'll tell Pat after I spend one last pleasant interlude with her. We don't have to send them on their way until just before dark."

"We? I thought you just said only a maniac would stay here to take on all those square-headed sons of bitches, Gaston."

Gaston shrugged and said, "I too think they are sons of bitches with square heads. We French owe them for 1870, as well as their more recent *très* disgusting butchery of women and children. I agree we are both behaving like maniacs. We shall probably both get killed. But what would I do for amusement in my declining years if I left you here alone to get killed? You are a *très* crazy bull-headed pain in the derriere, Dick Walker, but I never had such fun before I was mad enough to team up with you!"

Sylvia didn't want to go without him, but she sure enjoyed coming with him as they made love in his new hut, covered experimentally with slippery citronella oil. She asked how on earth she'd ever get it off, and he pointed out that she'd be able to enjoy a nice hot bath in Patuca after she contacted the British consulate there.

He said, "Just tell them there's a secret German base at Laguna Caratasca and they'll take over from there, honey. You and the others will be safe to leave for Blighty on the first steamer out. Not even Der Kaiser's spies in the field would be dumb enough to bother any of you once they knew you'd spilled the beans. They only murder people to keep them from singing. No point, after, and even a pro can only get away with so many murders, so . . ."

"I'm not worried about that, darling," she cut in, running her oily palms over his greasy buttocks as she thrust her pelvis up to take all his oiled shaft to the hilt. Her oily nipples sure felt neat against his chest. But though she went on screwing nicely she didn't seem to be as hot as expected. She asked, "Will we ever see each other again, Dick?"

He said, "Sure, you can write down your address in London for me before it's time to cut out."

She sobbed. "I know all too well how often you'll be getting to London! Can't you give up this perishing life, Dick? I've a good income and . . ."

"Don't talk dirty, just screw dirty," he cut in, adding, "There's a nasty word for a man who lets a woman support him. Besides, I'd need a British passport to be your kept lap dog, and those are kind of hard to apply for when a guy's wanted for everything but the common cold. Hey, I wonder what it would be like dog-style with all this slop on us."

"I don't feel acrobatic this afternoon, darling. I feel very left out of your life. Can't you just hold me tightly, like you never intend to let me go?"

He slid his hands down her oily buttocks to cup them as he got even deeper in her between her slippery, welcoming thighs. He didn't answer her question with words. It would have sounded dramatic to point out that he didn't know how much life he had left to leave her out of. Dames like her and guys like him had no business falling in love. So he tried not to as he made love to her.

It wasn't easy. Sylvia was beautiful as hell and a great lay, even without the added spice of the sensuous oil on her rippling curves. They came again. She begged for more. But he said, "I'd like to. I can't. By now the others are ready and must be sort of wondering, honey. We'd better get you dressed and on your way."

He climbed out of the hammock. She lay there, desirable as ever, with her eyes closed and a tear running down her oily cheek. She asked if he'd do her one last favor. He agreed, of course. She said, "I want you to get dressed first and just leave, Dick. I want you to go for a walk in the woods or something while I gather myself together. I'll be all right. I know what to do. But I'm afraid I'd act silly in front of the others if you were standing there as we drove off."

He bent, kissed her tear-filled eyelids, and ducked out of the hut without another word. Outside, he saw that Pat and the two Englishmen were waiting in the Stanley, with the fire already lit under the boiler. He waved to them and kept going until he was well out in the jungle. He sat down on a log in a copse of gumbo limbo and lit a smoke. The clothes he wore felt awful with all that grease on his body. He'd be able to dress as sensibly as the Indians, once the others left.

Come to think of it, now was as good a time as any to start. He stood up, peeled off his messed-up clothes, and sat down again, naked save for his boots and shoulder rig. It felt a lot better. It felt even better when little Decepcióna joined him on the log.

Decepcióna sat astride the smooth fallen timber, her freshly greased body facing him. Her legs of course were spread wide and her bare little box would get splinters in it if she wasn't careful. She said, "I followed you. Is it permitted?"

He said, "Of course," handing her the claro. She took a deep drag and handed it back, saying, "That is very good tobacco. I came to your hut to see if you wished anything. I went away when I saw you were making love to that *blanca*."

"Sorry about that, *querida*. I was, ah, saying goodbye to her."

"I understand. I could see why she was so upset to leave you behind. It upset me, too, a little. I am trying to understand why. The old ones say it is silly for a woman to want a man all to herself. Jealousy is a wicked vice. I am trying not to be jealous. It is not easy."

He twisted and sat facing her astride the log as he pulled her upper body closer. Their knees got in each other's way until the pragmatic Decepcióna solved the problem by slipping her greased thighs over his and sliding her little brown rump closer. He kissed her and said, "You don't have to be jealous anymore, if they've left."

She said, "They have. They drove off in the rolling choo-choo thing as I was leaving camp. Oh, my heart soars to feel what you still feel for me below the waist, Dick person. I did not think you would be able to do it again for some time, after the way I saw you bouncing on that *blanca* in the hammock. You are a very surprising man."

He too was pleasantly surprised to feel the head of his renewed enthusiasm throbbing teasingly between the oiled bare lips of her little brown box as she wriggled closer. The position was a bit awkward until he tossed the cigar away and wrapped both arms around her and pulled her in until her oiled torso and firm slippery breasts were against him. He knew they'd get messy as hell rolling in the soggy forest duff with all this oil on them. It was a novel position, too. So he stayed astride the log as he worked it in deeper. As a natural sex enthusiast who'd probably been at it since she could walk, Decepcióna caught on and pressed down with the backs of her thighs over his to raise her groin from the wood and slide all the way onto his shaft. She hissed in pleasure and started moving her widespread lap in his, saying, "Oh, this is nice! I've never done it this way before, have you?"

He assured her they were almost virgins, as he held her close and played pony boy with her. For a gal who said she was jealous, Decepcióna sure had a forgiving nature.

He realized why he was still up to it, as he mentally contrasted her with the more complicated white girl he'd just had. Decepcióna's face wasn't as pretty. Her body, while great, was too different to compare, so he couldn't judge who had the better shape. What he liked about his new love was that she didn't bullshit about love as they enjoyed good clean fun.

Sylvia had left him feeling guilty and gulpy-throated even as she'd screwed him silly. The mixed emotions had put him off his feed enough to keep him from really enjoying her to the full. This simple child of nature was making up for it in spades. She was literally screwing him with corkscrew motions of her shaved oily snatch, and, wonder of wonders, he was starting to come again!

She felt it as he ejaculated in her. She laughed and kept moving until he could tell by her contractions that she was coming, too. But, unlike most white women, she neither accused him of hurting her nor stopped what she was doing so nicely down there. She slipped out of his oiled arms to lean back with her back arched, her locked elbows holding her atop the log as she threw her head back and just enjoyed it with her eyes closed serenely and a pleased little smile on her face.

By the time she finished climaxing she had him hot as hell again. So he moved his legs back, leaned forward, and pressed her full length on the log to do it old-fashioned, sort of. As she locked her slippery legs around his waist, Decepcióna said calmly, "Don't let me fall off," so he said he wouldn't.

He held on to the log with his hands on either side of her trim waist as he leaned his upper body against her slithery brown breasts and braced a stiff leg out to either side for balance. As he started moving, entering her at an astounding angle, he wondered why he'd ever thought it was novel in a hammock. His well-braced hips were free to swivel in any direction, and did, as he long-donged her to mutual glory, kissing her sweet little mouth as his butt went crazy at a higher level. She'd caught on to kissing well by now, and tried to swallow his tongue alive as she did the same favor at the other end while he was coming in her.

When they had to stop, being only human, Decepcióna sighed contentedly and said, "I am glad that *blanca* is gone. Now I shall have you all to myself forever and you will be our new chief, no?"

He didn't answer. He'd just turned down an invitation to live the rest of his life in London. Apparently all women *were* sisters under the skin, no matter what color skin they wore.

It was a lousy shame. Men and women both deserved somebody who thought more like they did, but the Creator had fucked up both sexes when He'd created fucking, by giving them brains as different as the good parts. The only way a man or a woman could ever find a sex partner who thought the same way they did seemed sort of disgusting to a born heterosexual. It'd be fun to make it with an old pard who looked on life the same way, but he'd never met a man with she-male sex organs, so what the hell. He just had to grin and bear it.

He sat up, still astride the log and in her, to say, "We have to start thinking about this chief business. Will your warriors follow my orders to the letter, Decepcióna?"

"None of them can read letters, but they will do as you say, if I am there to translate, of course."

He hadn't thought of that. He said, "I don't want your pretty little ass any closer to those German field guns than they are right now, *niña mia!*"

She wriggled on his shaft teasingly and said, "I must come with you, if you wish the others to do as you say. And speaking of coming, Dick person . . ."

He started to say no. Then he wondered why any man would want to say a silly thing like that. He had some heavy planning to do. But he didn't have any office to do it in right now, and she sure could hold on well down there. He knew what she was deliberately doing with her skilled internal muscles to be able to hold an oil-slicked and half-soft erection in her at such an angle. It didn't stay half-soft long. He stayed upright astride the log, playing with her oily nipples as he started sliding his crotch back and forth on the now oil-polished-smooth mahogany. It sure beat doodling with a pad and pencil as he started to do some serious thinking about that German base.

Gaston must have been thinking along the same lines. He called out in English as he approached, *"Eh bien,* they've left for Patuca and Pat said she'd never forget or forgive me. So we have all these jolly Indians to ourselves and . . . Oops, I did not know you made friends so quickly, Dick!"

Decepcióna didn't seem at all embarrassed to be found in such a position, and it wasn't as if Captain Gringo and Gaston were strangers, but at least he stopped moving in her as he sat up to explain, "I've been working on a plan to do something about that base."

"*Oui,* I admire your grasp of strategy. Does she have a friend?"

Captain Gringo translated in Spanish for the Indian girl, adding that Gaston jerked off in public if he went more than a few hours without a woman. Gaston had just had a redhead young enough to be his granddaughter, but Decepcióna didn't know that. She said, "Oh, the poor thing. I can find him a woman as soon as we rejoin the others. If he's really suffering, I suppose I can take care of him right here. I am still most hot."

Captain Gringo grimaced as Gaston, who spoke better Spanish than either of them, laughed and said, "Move over and let a man show you how it is done, Dick!"

Captain Gringo looked down dubiously at the girl who was still holding his shaft in her and said, "I thought you were jealous, Decepcióna."

She said, "I am. I hate to see a pretty man making love to another woman. It makes me feel left out. I will not service your friend if you are jealous. It was just a suggestion."

Captain Gringo grimaced and said, "Go take a leak or something while I finish, and then she's all yours, pard. I see some practical advantages to not getting involved with more of these gals than we have to, even if it's a little disgusting."

"I don't like sloppy seconds any more than you do, dammit!" snapped Gaston in English. Captain Gringo translated, explaining that they'd better get another girl in deference to Gaston's sudden delicacy.

Decepcióna giggled and said, "I have an idea. It's something I have always wanted to try, and for some reason I can't seem to get enough today. Tell him not to go away. You lay flat on the log and let me get on top, Dick person."

He couldn't feel more silly, now. So he let her up to change places with him as Gaston watched, knowingly.

Decepcióna straddled the big Yank and the log to lower herself onto him again. It wouldn't have worked if she hadn't been so skilled, since now he was really beginning to lose interest and she had to work it in almost soft. She started milking it with her internal muscles as she lay down against him, her legs out to either side and her little brown butt raised high and wide. She started grinding her pubic bone in his oily pubic hair, teasing it up again as she explained, "If Gaston person gets behind me, he won't have to put it in the same place, no?"

Captain Gringo said, "Oh, for God's sake, this is getting *weird!*" as Gaston caught on, dropped his pants, and straddled the log behind her. Captain Gringo said, "It won't work, you crazy bastard! Haven't you any feelings? I'm about to come again, dammit. Go jerk off someplace!"

Gaston took Decepcióna's hips in his hands and shoved his own considerable tool up her rear as she gasped in pleased surprise. It felt wild as hell to all three of them. Captain Gringo's buttocks were pinned to the log by their combined weight and he couldn't thrust up and down, even though he was on the razor's edge of another orgasm.

He didn't have to. Between the amazing contractions of Decepcióna's vagina and Gaston's big tool sliding in and out on the other side of her thin internal partition, Captain Gringo was literally jerked off. He groaned as he came in her and said, "Let me *out* of here, dammit! This is getting close to a crime against nature! Stop it, Gaston! If I wanted to screw you I'd have done it a long time ago, you degenerate old fart!"

Neither of them listened. He'd beaten them to the punch and they were both too hot to stop if he'd put a gun to their heads. He slid out from between them and the greasy log to land on the damp duff on his bare butt. If they noticed, they didn't stop. He stood up to find his shirt and a smoke as Gaston pounded her to glory face down on the log. It took Gaston a while because he'd just been blown by Pat. It took Decepcióna a while because he was, after all, in the wrong hole. But by sliding her deserted love box on the oily mahogany she managed to come just before Gaston, who in turn rolled off to lay flat on his back in the muck, sighing, "Thank you, my children. It warms my heart to see how you respect your elders."

Captain Gringo said, "Put your fucking pants back on if you don't want to wear grease. Enough of this bullshit. We've got a German base to take out and this isn't the way to do it!"

It turned out that Decepcióna did have a girl for Gaston back at the village. So, since the horny old fart had only spilled his seed in a part Captain Gringo hadn't figured on using anyway, he decided to forgive them.

Her free and easy ways eliminated any future guilt he might feel when they left the Indians, as he knew they must. Meanwhile, as she was the only dame in the band he could talk to, he decided to keep going steady with her, if that was the right term. After she'd cooled off, even Decepcióna realized she'd been a little bit naughty and said she wouldn't lay anyone else without his permission, even if he was asleep.

So they slept. Most of them. Captain Gringo sent a couple of eager young warriors out to do some scouting in the dark. He knew they could case the base and get back to him before noon the next day. He knew where the damned base was. He just had no idea of the layout. He told his scouts not to go into business for themselves with their six-foot hardwood bows, explaining that he wanted his own visit to be a surprise.

After sundown and a shared supper of tinned bully beef and beans with Decepcióna, Gaston, and Gaston's new girl, a skinny little thing with a lot of *x*s in her unpronounceable Indian name, Captain Gringo ordered a good night's sleep all around. He added, "I mean it, Gaston. I know you like to explore new territory. So do I. But don't wear yourself out on Miss X. She doesn't have to run like a deer *mañana*. You and I may have to."

Gaston said he understood, that he'd decided to call her Mimi in honor of another brunette he knew, and that he'd only go around the world with her once.

Decepcióna had hung her own hammock in Captain Gringo's new hut. The Indians knew all too well that while two people could screw in one hammock, sleeping double in them was out of the question. That was fine with him. He'd thought after that orgy in the jungle that he'd had enough of her for now. But they did a little commuting anyhow when the mosquitoes woke them up despite the citronella oil in the wee small hours and he saw that, while he had a morning hard-on, it was too late to bother going back to sleep. Decepcióna said she was glad she was forgiven, when they played swing in her hammock.

But he husbanded his strength by ejaculating in her only once and insisting on an early breakfast. She accepted this as she accepted all life's pleasures. She wasn't used to English rations, and since on the other hand she knew all there was to know about sex, the bully beef and canned peas this time offered her new sensual pleasures to explore.

Later, Gaston found him sitting bare-assed in Bertie's remaining car, listening to the headset he'd taken from the patrol leader. Gaston joined him, oiled, naked, and looking a little bushed. As Gaston literally slid into the leather seat beside him, he asked what he was listening to.

Captain Gringo said, "Dots and dashes. Sounds like International Morse. But they must be transmitting in German. I haven't any idea what. Here, see if you can make it out."

Gaston pressed an earphone to his head, listened awhile, and said, "It's German. But in code. 'My mother's hound says the cabbage is lavender' can't mean anything but a code. It's not a cypher. The triple-thumbed species of ham-handed pig-shit eater is using senseless but whole words. To decode it, one would need the code book. I don't suppose you looked for any?"

"I did. I didn't find it. Besides, I don't think Bertie was a German. Just a hungry Englishman. They're probably sending to a patrol they put out to survey the damage back where they shelled us. We ought to be okay here for a while. By the way, it's not pig *shit* they eat. Germans eat pigs' *feet*, Gaston."

"That, too. Don't tell me they don't eat shit. You were not there in 1870. The German who is not eating your shit is shitting in your face. They have very predictable habits."

"I didn't know you fought in the Franco-Prussian war, Gaston. I thought after you deserted the Legion in Mexico, back in the late sixties . . ."

"Haven't you ever heard of a *boat?* I don't boast of my service at Sedan. The idiot we had for a leader surrendered. I found it *très fatigue* in that Prussian prison camp, so of course I went back to Mexico, where one has some chance of predicting the outcome when one signs up to fight. *Merde alors,* the government France had, then, got a lot of poor peasant boys killed while the officers drank and fornicated miles from the front. The next war France has with the Boche will be different."

"I hope you're right. Wars keep getting messier as this century winds down. Nobody had machine guns or long-range artillery in our Civil War, yet it was bloody enough. Hate to think what an officer like Burnside or even Grant would do with green troops ordered into a bayonet charge against modern weapons."

*"Oui,* this radio business seems a disturbing complication, too. In the good old days one had to consider only the species of enemy out in front of one's positions. Now, even if you seem to be winning, you must worry about the sons of the bitch calling for assistance by wireless! Listen, Dick, do you think we could send amusing messages to the Boche with the transmitter in this vehicle? It might be *très amuse, non?"*

"Yeah, and it would tell them we're still alive and still within transmitting range, too! I think there's a way to pin down the location of a transmitter, too. I don't think we'd better wire that the Kaiser is a shit-for-brains just yet. Let them figure it out for themselves."

Later, near noon, the Indian youths he'd sent out to scout returned. Decepcióna brought them to Captain Gringo and Gaston and translated as they drew a map in the red clay for them.

It was a pretty good map, considering that they were supposed to be stupid savages. Their outline of the huge lagoon matched the one on paper pretty well, and he knew they couldn't just have completed a circuit of the fifty-mile body of water. He knew they had a lot of it in their heads, since it was their country, after all.

The Indians verified that there was a gun emplacement out on the south point forming an almost shut entrance to the lagoon. The main camp was nowhere near the old pirate camp. Wallace had been bullshitting.

The scouts put it at the base of the south peninsula hemming in the lagoon. Captain Gringo nodded and told Gaston, "Makes sense. From that position they have an inland anchorage to their west and a view of the open sea to their east. They probably like to watch the boats go by. Decepcióna, ask if they saw any vessels at anchor in the lagoon. Big boats. Gray. Maybe little cigar-shaped boats with a tower in the middle of a long deck?"

Decepcióna did. They said the harbor was empty. He nodded and told Gaston, "It's a supply dump, then. They must not plan a war this season. The idea is to set up a supply-and-communications base near the Panama Canal, for later."

*"Eh bien,* that means later indeed, Dick. The canal is not half-completed yet. It may never be, thanks to the confused politics down that way."

"It will be. If Colombia won't be sensible about it, sooner or later Uncle Sam or Queen Vickie figures to just *grab* the canal zone. That canal's too vital to anyone with a two-ocean navy to let the pig-headed Colombian junta hold things up much longer."

Gaston shrugged as he stared down morosely at the scratched out diagram and said, "To hell with the coming century. Let's live through the rest of *this* one! Our Boche friends have done a nice job, for eaters of pig shit. Regard how they are dug in with the sea protecting them on three sides. To winkle them out would take a *très* desperate charge by a lot of *très* suicidal troops against that one narrow front they have to worry about."

Captain Gringo got Decepcióna to ask the scouts about the landward approaches up the narrow peninsula. She did, and told them, "They were afraid to go very close. Mangroves and other trees grow on that spit of land, all the way out to the tip, except where the bad *blancos* have cleared in places. They have piled bags filled with something in a waist-high wall across the peninsula from water's edge to water's edge. But the ends are hidden by piled brush. Between the wall of bags and the land, they have dug a ditch and they have some of that nasty wire the Spanish use to fence in banana plantations lately. Our boys of course slip through the sharp wire easily. But these warriors say the bad *blancos* have strung it very thickly, in more than one line."

Captain Gringo grunted and said, "That's a neat one I've heard before. Firing line of sandbags, guarded by a dry moat and barbed wire. Did you ever get the feeling you weren't welcome somewhere, Gaston?"

"Bah, given a brigade of my old Legion and an hour or so's barrage to soften them up, I could get through. The two of us and a dozen unwashed archers is another matter, however!"

"Yeah, when you're right you're right. There has to be a better way."

He checked the Indian's outline against his more accurate navigational chart and said, "Okay, that battery of eight-inchers is out on the point, a good ten miles or more from the main base across the south end of the peninsula. They might have a wire strung to talk to mother. But how fast can anyone run ten miles?"

Gaston said, "Too fast, if you mean to spend much time out on the tip of that adorable spit. But are we not forgetting that to get out to the end of the peninsula, one must first go through the defenses at the base?"

"I wish you wouldn't be such a party pooper. Wallace said there was a gun emplacement on both sides of the lagoon entrance. On the other hand, Wallace screwed his friends' wives, then screwed his friends. Decepcióna, ask them if there could be more big guns on the north point."

Decepcióna did. They said they didn't know. Gaston said the question about the north point was academic, adding, "To get there, one would have to circle the great lagoon. It would take days."

Captain Gringo said, "No, it wouldn't. That's what the wheel was invented for. It may call for some heavy machete work. But the terrain is flat and if we started now we'd get there just before dawn."

Gaston rolled his eyes heavenward and said, "Then what, you maniac? Even if one assumes the north point is not guarded, the south point lies across at least two miles of water, and we know they have big guns dug in!"

Captain Gringo didn't answer. He was thinking. He had watched the Indians long enough to know who was good with a machete. They'd have to leave most of the men to look after the women and children here. But the tribe could probably spare four guys and Decepcióna, if he promised not to lose them. The two scouts here would insist on going. That meant he needed two really husky machete swingers and, yeah, there might be room for one good tom-tom man. When he asked the girl who their best drummer was, Gaston snorted, "Now I know he's crazy! It's not enough he wishes to attack a military base the hard way. Now he wants to announce our approach with some species of idiot beating on a goddamn drum!"

They stopped just before sunset and Captain Gringo ordered everyone out of the steam car to stretch their legs. Gaston said it was about time. He'd insisted on bringing his "Mimi" along, which only seemed fair. So they'd been a little crowded, with the two naked Indian girls having to take turns riding in Gaston's lap. Gaston hadn't minded that part.

As the two female and five male Indians automatically started to build another small town, he told Decepcióna to forget it as he opened the car's repair kit. He found a coil of bailing wire and sent an Indian up a tree with it to tie one end to a branch and drop the rest of the long thin wire down to him. Then as Gaston watched, bemused, Captain Gringo started taking the car apart. Gaston said, "The steamer was running well enough, if one ignores a broken spine. What on earth are you doing?"

Captain Gringo crawled under the chassis with his tools as he explained in a somewhat muffled voice, "Taking out the radio gear. Get a screw driver and start working on the battery mounts up front. Don't bust any wires, though."

Gaston shrugged and said he had nothing better to do. So in less than a quarter of an hour they had the battery and the transmitter that had been hidden by the dash laid out neatly on the grass, still connected by a confusion of wires. Captain Gringo had left the generator in place under the chassis after merely disconnecting it.

He told Decepcióna to bring the tribal drummer over, and as she did so he explained to Gaston, "We're out of artillery range now. Hopefully we're still close enough to the base for them to pick up an S.O.S."

"We wish to call on Germany for help, Dick?"

"Not exactly. They'll assume we've discovered the Marconi stuff and that we're yelling for help to the world in general. If they range on the direction of the signals, they'll assume we're stuck here. The guys who deserted us will have told them we were low on kerosene. We've made hash out of two of their patrols. So they won't order them to head for this spot after dark. But our tom-tom guy had better move his ass before the sun comes up again."

Decepcióna brought the drummer over and translated as Captain Gringo told the frowning Indian what he wanted him to do. The Indian said he could surely keep tapping the funny little key in the same rhythm of three dots and three dashes from time to time through the night, with time off to pee or jerk off. But he didn't see why.

Captain Gringo told his pretty translatress, "Tell him it's big medicine to fool the spirits of the bad *blancos*. We'll leave him here with plenty of food and water. At first light he must stop and head back to the others at your new camp. Tell him to swing wide. Bad men may be coming this way."

She did, and the drummer agreed to the plan, even if he didn't understand it. A few minutes later they were steaming on through the jungle.

Gaston nodded and said, "*Oui,* it ought to work. If they pinpoint us on the map back there, they will not expect us to turn up anywhere else. Naturally, they will assume the others are still with us and that both cars have run out of fuel, *non?*"

"Right. If one car was still rolling, the bunch of us could have driven on in the survivor, crowded or not. The ruse gives Sylvia and the others an added margin of safety, too. There's no sense radioing possible pals in Patuca to watch for 'em if they don't think any of us made it halfway there!"

"I don't mind riding crowded," said Gaston, grinning as he leaned back to close his eyes while Mimi bounced on his lap more than the slow rolling really called for. Captain Gringo chuckled and asked, "Have you got your dong in that dame, you old goat?"

"Where else would I have it? You asked me not to do it to your girl anymore."

"Okay, but try not to overdo it. We need to save our strength."

He braked to a stop and consulted his map by the rapidly fading light. Then he nodded and said, "Okay, we're making good time. If we don't drive down an alligator's mouth in the dark, we should make it well before the next time we see daylight."

They didn't see any 'gators or much of anything else that night, but it was really rough going. Thanks to steam power, they made it through patches of hub-deep muck that an internal-combustion or electric car would have been stuck in for keeps. The muscular machete men had their work cut out for them as from time to time they had to hack a quarter mile or more through tangled vegetation.

By 4:00 A.M. Captain Gringo had emptied the last reserves of citronella oil into the main fuel tank and couldn't come up with an answer when Gaston asked how in hell they were going to drive back the other way. Gaston bitched, *"Merde,* I foresee a long weary walk to Patuca, if we live that long."

They had to be near the tip of the peninsula they'd driven out on by now. So Captain Gringo sent his two scouts ahead as he turned down the oil fire to conserve fuel. Decepcióna suggested a walk in the woods while they waited. He told her not to talk dirty as he got to work mounting the machine gun on the hood with the action hanging back over the dash so that he could man both the steering wheel and the trigger from his seat. He put the last extra ammo canisters on the floorboards between the two front seats and wedged them good with whittled wooden stakes.

Then there was nothing to do but wait. A million years later the two scouts came back, grinning like naughty boys. Decepcióna said, "They say there was a small how you say outpost out on the tip of this point. Two bad *blancos* were there with a spy glass and a tom-tom-tom gun like this one."

"*Bueno*. Did the Germans see them?"

"No. They saw the German persons first. They put arrows in them and cut off their heads."

One of the archers held up something dark and dripping in the dim light. Captain Gringo whistled softly and said, "Remind me never to shell a Mosquito village. Okay, that doesn't give us much time. They'll probably be rowing across to change the guard at the outpost as soon as it's light. Get everybody back in, Decepcióna. We have to get out of there *poco tiempo*."

As he turned up the fire and opened the throttle, Gaston asked, "Is there any point to driving farther, Dick? She just told you they took out the outpost."

"I heard her. We have to get across the straits of the lagoon before it's too light."

"In a steam car? You can't ford two or more miles of salt water on wheels, dammit! The passage is deep enough for oceangoing vessels to enter!"

"Yeah, small ones, anyway. They're probably figuring on submersibles when the big one starts in a decade or so."

He saw a break in the trees ahead. He stopped a moment to tell his girl to put the machete men to work, adding that he wanted balsa logs if possible.

Gaston bitched, but couldn't help grinning wolfishly as he said, "I don't know why I listen to this foolish child, *mon Dieu*. Who ever heard of attacking a dug-in gun battery with a balsa raft!"

Captain Gringo said, "Nobody. That's why they shouldn't be expecting it. They think they have an outpost on this side. Will you take your dong out of Mimi and *help*, Goddamn it?"

A little over an hour later, as the sky began to pearl pinkly above the eastern sea horizon, a German marine sentry noticed a dark smudge out on the closer waters of the lagoon entrance. He couldn't make out what it was. It was probably another drifting mat of vegetation drifting out to sea with the tide. But a good German wasn't paid to think for himself. His standing orders were to report all unusual occurences on or near his post to the corporal of the guard. So he walked south beyond the two big eight-inch Howitzers and ducked into the noncom's sandbagged tent to wake his superior. The corporal of the guard had been enjoying a wet dream and sat up with a groan and a curse, growling, *"Zum teuffel*, what is it, Dorfler?"

"There is something out on the water, Herr Korporal. I thought you'd want to know."

*"Herr Gott!* It's still dark out and I was about to come in that big blonde! Has the outpost across the strait phoned anything in?"

*"Nein.* But it could be a native raft putting out to sea from somewhere else, Herr Korporal."

"Heading for the open sea? *Gross Gott* let me go back to sleep, you idiot."

The sentry shrugged and ducked back outside. Then the noncom rubbed a hand across his sleep-drugged face and said, "Wait. You'd better show it to me. The old man will have my ass for breakfast if we let anything fuck up this mission even worse. The officers are giving birth to cows over that crazy American with the machine gun."

As he pulled on his pants and boots he added, "Americans have no sense of proportion. He was not supposed to shoot *us* up. We were supposed to shoot him and his Britisher friends up. Fortunately, they now seem stuck in the jungles across the lagoon. The signalman phoned a little while ago that they are sending distress calls with the radio equipment they were not supposed to know about."

The two Germans left the tent and headed for the north shore. Others had been awakened by the commotion and were stepping out of the other tents, yawning and asking what was up. The corporal told a gunnery sergeant to go back to sleep. It was probably nothing.

Then, as he neared the water's edge and saw Captain Gringo's raft grounding on the coral sand with a steam car filled with naked people already rolling forward, he managed one good scream before a burst of machine-gun fire blew his lungs out his back and sent the sentry at his side sprawling dead without ever knowing what had hit him!

Gaston had the German machine-gun from the outpost braced in front of him, as well, as the two soldiers of fortune drove up the sloping beach into the gun emplacement, both firing full automatic. The Indians, as planned, rolled out and hit the deck.

The nice thing about the two big guns being dug in behind sandbag walls to seaward and landward was that there was only one direction anyone could run. So Gaston swiveled in his passenger seat to hose the bottleneck as Captain Gringo drove in tight circles, mowing down anything dead ahead and rolling over the wounded with his hard rubber tires until the belt was used up. As he stopped to reach down for a fresh belt, Gaston put a good burst into the knot of moaning Germans piled up on the road south and ceased fire. The Indians leaped to their feet and joined the fun and games, using their machetes and poison arrows on a lot of people who probably would have died anyway.

Captain Gringo finished reloading the Maxim and said, "Come on, Gaston. It's time you earned all the ass I've been getting you. You know where the base camp is, and I just got you a couple of eight-inch guns. Can do?"

"I can aim and fire. But those big shells and eighty-pound powder charges are a bit much for a man of my advanced senility, Dick!"

"Get Decepcióna and the Indians to help you load. They're quick pupils. Pile out, dammit. I'll cover you with these two machine guns!"

Gaston drew his revolver and rolled out to run toward the guns, stark naked save for grease as he bellowed for Decepcióna to get her adorable bare ass over to him. The sight must have been very distressing to a badly wounded German just sitting up. He screamed. Gaston blew his face off and kept going, muttering, "Silly Boche!"

Captain Gringo drove the steamer over other Germans to where the sandbags formed wings on either side of the service road to the main base. He braked to a stop and made sure there was a fresh belt for the Spandau, too. It was getting lighter by the minute and he could see almost a quarter of a mile down the road. It formed a sort of tunnel between the trees the Germans had left on either side for camouflage.

He winced as Gaston fired one of the big eight-inchers behind him to send a shell screaming south. A second ear-splitting detonation whipped his bare back with its shock wave sooner than he'd expected. How the hell could even Gaston reload and fire so fast? Oh, right, the old artillery ace was using both guns, letting the Indians manhandle the heavy ammo on one as he fired the other. Pretty slick. Ouch! There he went again, and the first shells were already landing with duller roars a dozen miles or so to the south. If Gaston was aiming as good as he was firing, the base camp was in big trouble!

Farther out to sea, the commanding officer of the U.S.S. *Maine* was out on the bridge wing, staring shoreward as he listened to the distant thunder of big guns. A junior officer joined him to say, "Sparks says he's still picking up that S.O.S., sir. It seems to be coming from the mainland. It can't be another vessel in distress as we thought."

The skipper said, *"Somebody's* in trouble. Listen to those big guns on the horizon. Order Captain Gates to get his marines ready. We'd best send in a landing party."

The junior officer frowned and said, "Ay ay, sir. But, ah, Honduras is supposed to be a friendly country."

"So I hear. I hear big guns, too. The U.S.S. *Maine* is cruising these waters to keep the peace, mister. And I mean to keep the Mosquito Coast peaceful if I have to kill every one of the damned greasers. The Honduran military isn't allowed to have bigger guns than the U.S. Marines. If some sons of bitches have armed the rebel faction with eight-inchers, Uncle Sam is going to be mad as hell about it. Get those marines ready to go ashore and restore order with their Krags, dammit! You have your orders. Any questions about 'em?"

"Just one, sir. What if they train those big guns on us as we steam in?"

"What? Fire on the U.S.S. *Maine!* Unthinkable, mister. Nobody nicks the paint of the *Maine* if they don't want a war they'll remember!"

On shore, Captain Gringo was blissfully unaware of the hornets' nest he'd stirred up with his radio signals meant to confuse the Germans. But he had other troubles. It was almost broad daylight now, and a mess of white-clad German marines were boiling up the road from the south on the double, rifles at port as they jogged in perfect step.

They spotted him at about the same time, slid to a stop, and spread out to take cover in the trees on either side. He growled, "Nice going, you poor dumb assholes. Didn't your mothers ever tell you that mangroves don't grow thick enough to stop a bullet?"

He crouched down, held the grips of one machine gun in each hand, and opened up with plunging fire, moving the two streams of hot lead like a giant pair of garden shears as he traversed blindly but effectively at maximum range.

He ceased fire when he saw some guys way down the road, running like hell the other way. There weren't too many of them. He grinned and reloaded both machine guns, just in case some wise-ass was still brave enough to try to move in on his belly through the brush.

Nothing happened for a while. Gaston had stopped firing. A few minutes later the Frenchman joined him, followed by the sweated-up but grinning Indians. Gaston said, *"Eh bien*. I expended every shell on hand, and if I did not flatten that German base, I most certainly worried the *merde* out of them! Let us return to the raft and get our adorable asses out of here. We can drop our friends off at the north base of the peninsula, put our pants back on, and be in Patuca in no time."

They all piled in. Captain Gringo opened the throttle and drove south down the service road, saying, "Watch the trees on either side. You never know when some wounded snake in the grass will be a poor loser."

"Dick, you are going the *wrong way,* dammit!"

"No, I'm not. Even if we had the fuel to make Patuca, which we don't, it'd still be a piss-poor place for two wanted men to turn up. By now Sylvia and the others have made it to the British consulate in Patuca. Said consulate will have told the Honduran authorities there's a mess of trespassers on Honduran soil. I don't want to shoot it out with the Honduran army if I don't have to, do you?"

*"Mais non,* we trained some of them a while back, as I recall! But where can we go?"

"Depends on what we find at the main German base. Decepcióna, tell your friends to bail out and run into the trees when I slow down. It won't be long now. I see a break in the cover up ahead."

So the Indians rolled over the sides a few minutes later and Captain Gringo opened the throttle wide to drive into the German camp lickety split, both machine guns firing wildly as they bounced over shell craters Gaston's barrage had left all over the place. Flattened wreckage and bodies lay all around, and a screaming German ran out from behind some stacked cases waving a white pillowcase in a gesture of surrender. Gaston snarled, "Surely you jest!" and chopped him down with a burst of Spandau fire.

Captain Gringo slid to a stop by a pile of fuel drums. He said, "Cover me while I refill our empty cans. Don't shoot any more poor bastards who want to give up, Gaston."

"You get the diesel oil and let *me* deal with Boche! You were not there when they fired on our white flag in '70, Dick."

Nobody else showed his or her face as Captain Gringo got the diesel oil. When they had enough, he put his fingers between his lips and whistled for Decepcióna and the other Indians. They came running. As they leaped a shell crater and were passing a downed German marine, he made the mistake of raising his head. One of the machete men lopped it off without breaking stride.

They piled into the steamer. Captain Gringo opened the throttle again and spun a cloud of sand behind them as he revved the wheels with the throttle wide open. So they were doing about forty miles an hour when he hit the sandbag parapet south of the base, plowed through it to bounce over the dry moat, and tore through the barbed wire as if it hadn't been there. As he slowed down to steer between the trees of uncut jungle to the south, he mused aloud, "That's the answer to barbed wire. Remind me to write a letter to my congressman if we ever have a war with Germany."

"I don't think they will listen, Dick. Your loving Uncle Sam still wants to hang you. Will you tell me, now, where we are going?"

"Back to Puerto Cabezas. We can drop our redskin pals off at the next westbound trail."

They were speaking English, so Decepcióna still didn't know the honeymoon was over. Gaston said, *"Eh bien,* I've exhausted my imagination trying to think up some way to make zigzig with Mimi. Do I have time to screw Decepcióna right, if you're through with her?"

"No. We couldn't have killed everybody back there, even though you did one hell of a swell job. I want to get a good start on any pissed-off survivors. I don't want to be around when anyone else comes along to mop up, either. They could have heard your cannonade up in Patuca if the wind was right."

"*Eh bien,* I agree Patuca might not have a healthy climate for two wanted men at the moment. But have you forgotten they are hunting us in Puerto Cabezas as well?"

"No, they're not. The last time the cops there saw us, we were tearing ass out of town in a horseless carriage. We'll ditch this in a swamp before we get there, then walk in under cover of darkness, looking innocent as hell. We know better than to head for Fifi's again. But the posada Sylvia picked me up in should be safe until we can find a boat headed for Costa Rica. The barkeep who called the cops is dead. Nobody else there could have sicced the cops on me. The cops don't make a habit of sweeping that part of town."

They drove on until they came to a place in what looked like virgin jungle that the scouts recognized. Neither white man could see how, but it was their jungle, and if they said the invisible path led back to their people, they had to be right.

With Decepcióna's help, he got them all out and headed for home. The men started west without comment. But the two girls said they wanted to say goodbye properly. Gaston grinned, took Decepcióna's arm, and asked, "Dick?"

Captain Gringo sighed and said, "How soon they forget. Okay, I have to refill the main tank, anyway. But make it a quicky."

Gaston started leading Decepcióna into the trees as she asked him, innocently, "Is not Dick person coming too?"

"*Mais non, mon petite.* This time I mean to discover for myself if you are as tight up front as you are behind. Come say goodbye to your Uncle Gaston like a good little girl."

Captain Gringo grunted in annoyance as he refilled the steamer's tank. He knew he was dumb to feel annoyed. Decepcióna had been the kind of dame every man said he was looking for, until he found one. It was a shame you couldn't meet a dedicated sex maniac who was devoted to you alone.

He tossed away the empty tin and moved around to the seats, wondering if he should start thinking of getting dressed again. The oil on his naked skin was almost all rubbed off by now, and people might talk if he went into town bare-assed.

He saw that Mimi had climbed into the backseat and was reclining against the cushions with her thighs spread invitingly as she smiled mutely at him. He said, "You're a pretty little thing, too. I've always admired skinny dames with big tits, but, Jesus, haven't you had enough yet?"

The Indian girl of course had no idea what he was saying and couldn't talk to him. But she put her fingers to the slit of her oiled, shaved pubis in a gesture that needed no words. So Captain Gringo grinned and said, "Oh, hell, since you put it that way . . ." as he climbed in the backseat with her, already rising to the occasion.

Mimi took his dawning erection in hand to guide it into her as he added, "We've probably got time for a quicky. Gaston will take forever with a new partner and . . ." Then, as he felt what he was getting into, he thrust hard and groaned, "Oh, yeah, let's hope Gaston takes at least a couple of *hours* getting back!"

# The Best of Adventure
# by RAMSAY THORNE

# 5 EXCITING ADVENTURE SERIES MEN OF ACTION BOOKS

___NINJA MASTER
*by Wade Barker*
Committed to avenging injustice, Brett Wallace uses the ancient Japanese art of killing as he stalks the evildoers of the world in his mission.

___#5 BLACK MAGICIAN (C30-178, $1.95)
___#7 SKIN SWINDLE (C30-227, $1.95)
___#8 ONLY THE GOOD DIE (C30-239, $2.25, U.S.A.)
(C30-695, $2.95, Canada)


___THE HOOK
*by Brad Latham*
Gentleman detective, boxing legend, man-about-town, The Hook crossed 1930's America and Europe in pursuit of perpetrators of insurance fraud.

___#1 THE GILDED CANARY (C90-882, $1.95)
___#2 SIGHT UNSEEN (C90-841, $1.95)
___#5 CORPSES IN THE CELLAR (C90-985, $1.95)


___S-COM
*by Steve White*
High adventure with the most effective and notorious band of military mercenaries the world has known—four men and one woman with a perfect track record.

___#3 THE BATTLE IN BOTSWANA (C30-134, $1.95)
___#4 THE FIGHTING IRISH (C30-141, $1.95)
___#5 KING OF KINGSTON (C30-133, $1.95)


___BEN SLAYTON: T-MAN
*by Buck Sanders*
Based on actual experiences, America's most secret law-enforcement agent—the troubleshooter of the Treasury Department—combats the enemies of national security.

___#1 A CLEAR AND PRESENT DANGER (C30-020, $1.95)
___#2 STAR OF EGYPT (C30-017, $1.95)
___#3 THE TRAIL OF THE TWISTED CROSS (C30-131, $1.95)
___#5 BAYOU BRIGADE (C30-200, $1.95)


___BOXER UNIT—OSS
*by Ned Cort*
The elite 4-man commando unit of the Office of Strategic Studies whose dare-devil missions during World War II place them in the vanguard of the action.

___#3 OPERATION COUNTER-SCORCH (C30-128, $1.95)
___#4 TARGET NORWAY (C30-121, $1.95)

# "THE KING OF THE WESTERN NOVEL" IS *MAX BRAND*

# DIRTY HARRY
## by DANE HARTMAN

**Never before published or seen on screen.**

He's "Dirty Harry" Callahan—tough, unorthodox, no-nonsense plain-clothesman extraordinaire of the San Francisco Police Department...Inspector #71 assigned to the bruising, thankless homicide detail...A consummate crimebuster nothing can stop—not even the law!